LOOK AGAIN

A NOVELLA

MARLISS MELTON

A Notice To The Reader/Limit Of Liability/ Disclaimer Of Warranty:

This book is a work of fiction and is a product of the author's imagination or is used fictitiously. Names, characters, and incidents in this book have no existence outside the imagination of the author and have no relation whatsoever to anyone, living or dead, bearing the same name or names. All incidents are pure invention from the author's imagination. Any resemblance to actual events or locales or persons, living or dead, is entirely coincidental.

First James-York Press Print edition: June 2014

JAMES-YORK PRESS
P. O. Box 141
Williamsburg, VA 23187

Edited by Sydney Baily-Gould
Cover Design by Dar Albert Logo by Chauncey Burgazli
Layout by BB Ebooks

ISBN: 978-1-938732-14-0 e-book
ISBN: 978-1-938732-15-7 paperback

CHAPTER ONE

I'M BEING WATCHED.

A familiar tingle raced from Katie Crowley's fingertips to the top of her head, raising the hairs on the back of her neck. The last time she'd felt it had been outside her home two days ago as she stood on her doorstep and realized that her house had been broken into. That same creepy feeling had just come over her again in the middle of the pet food aisle in Food Lion.

Swiveling her head, she glimpsed a wisp of movement at the far end of the aisle as a tall figure darted out of view.

Is it my imagination?

It just might be. An episode that had occurred nearly a decade ago had left her with Post Traumatic Stress Disorder that had taken years to subdue.

That PTSD might have made a return last week when she'd come home to find her kenneled dogs in an uproar and the glass pane in her front door shattered. The perpetrator had apparently fled at the sound of her return, but she'd sensed him lurking close enough to watch her reaction to the broken glass, the turned lock.

Since the incident, she'd seen the same dark beater of a car in her rearview mirror trailing her SUV from a distance. And now her stalker had followed her into the store. Or had he? Her heart thudded as she hurried up the aisle, her grocery list forgotten.

She'd reported the attempted break-in to her uncle, the county sheriff, who'd attributed the vandalism to a troubled teen living down the road. If she told him of her present fears, he'd certainly think she was overreacting. Perhaps she was. Nosing her cart into the next aisle, she drew up short.

Halfway down the aisle, a tall stranger blocked her path. Her gaze locked on him. The aisle was wide enough for the two of them, but six feet and several inches of pure testosterone had her gripping her cart so hard her knuckles ached.

Her lungs had trouble seizing air. He didn't move. With his back to her, he regarded the protein shakes on the shelf. She was not imagining the aura of danger that radiated from his broad shoulders, projected in part by the muscular arms jutting from his sleeveless T-shirt. Thick black hair in need of a comb concealed his neck. As he turned his head to study the various brands of liquid nutrition, she spied an unkempt beard.

This man was too wrapped up in his shopping to be her stalker, she decided.

Braced for the least sign of hostility, Katie proceeded forward. The man's T-shirt and shorts looked like he'd slept in them. He took a six-pack of protein shakes off the shelf, dropped it in his basket and headed away from her, limping as he pushed his cart. Katie's gaze dropped to his feet. The man wore a prosthetic foot, strapped to his left ankle.

Wariness melted into curiosity as she watched him swivel toward the checkout lines. The barest glimpse of his profile brought a gasp of recognition to her lips. Was that her old high-school crush, Tyler Rexall?

The glow of warmth that his name engendered faded abruptly as she realized what Tyler's return to Louisa meant. The former high-school football star and hometown hero had been gone for the last ten years. Everybody knew he was a US Navy SEAL. On a brief visit home a few years back, he'd been offered a spot in the Christmas parade riding on a float with the current football team. The whole town had turned out to cheer him for his service to the country. Whenever the SEALs were credited in the media for slowing the tide of terror, the hearts of Louisa County residents beat with patriotic fervor because Tyler was one of them.

Until now. His current physical appearance suggested an appalling circumstance: His glory days were over.

Stunned and utterly dismayed for him, Katie trailed after him, her earlier fears forgotten. She caught sight of him again piling his purchases onto the conveyer belt at checkout three. Slowing her step, she gave herself ample time to examine her conclusions.

Was it really Tyler? His classically handsome face, always open and inviting, looked haggard and closed. Jet-black eyebrows formed a V over his deep-set eyes. His mouth, buried in the beard that furred his jaw, was crimped with either pain or irritability. Stark cheekbones and a body that was all brawn and bone testified to recent weight loss. Still, there was no mistaking his devastating good looks or the breadth of his shoulders. It was Tyler; only he'd changed, and no wonder.

Would he remember her if she said hello?

She'd never counted him among her friends in high school, but not for lack of trying. Tyler was older by a year. His popularity with both the staff and the students was something a pudgy nerd like her could only dream about. As their all-star quarterback, he'd earned Louisa High School football team their one and only state championship.

He might remember Katie from their few advanced classes together, but he'd never given her the time of day, so probably not. Besides, his expression was as inviting as a lit stick of dynamite.

He looked up suddenly, catching her staring. Not a flicker of recognition brightened the lusterless quality of his whisky-colored eyes, so Katie looked away, shifting her attention to a sign behind him. Then she ducked into the soda aisle, feeling insignificant. By the time she glanced back, he was gathering his purchases and limping out of the store.

I could help him, she realized. There wasn't any question as to why. Recalling the glowing, confident being he'd been before, it was simply unacceptable to see him beaten down. Plus, at last, there was something that she—Katie Crowley—could do for him that he couldn't do for himself.

The only problem was that he would refuse her offer of help, she was certain. Most of her clients had to hit rock bottom before they acknowledged their need for a service dog. The intrepid T-Rex, as he'd been dubbed in high school, would probably rather kill himself than admit to any weakness.

But she wasn't going to let that fact impede her. Oh, no. The scowl of defeat on Tyler's face plucked at every heartstring. Therefore, even if it meant telling him some white lies, she would get him to take the dog she had in mind.

Making life easier for people—that was what she did. Actually, the dogs did that. Katie just trained them.

Ensconced in a recliner in the TV room of his parents' ten-bedroom farmhouse, Tyler flipped through the dismal array of channels. His parents had finally gotten cable, but they'd obviously opted for the cheapest package. The only programs on TV in the middle of the day were reruns of *Friends*, and the lineups on CNN, HGTV, and ESPN. He would have been content to watch the latter, except that golf had never captured his interest. The only reason it was even a sport, in his opinion, was that, aside from whacking a little white ball into a hole, it required a lot of walking—which meant he couldn't even play fucking golf if he wanted to.

Disgusted, Tyler shut off the TV and let the silence of his parents' estate surround him. He hadn't come here looking for solitude, not really. He'd come for the solace of his mother's voice, only she wasn't there. She wasn't anywhere, actually. A victim of dementia, she'd been moved to the nursing facility fifteen minutes up the road in Gordonsville. She hadn't even recognized him when he'd gone to visit.

His father, every bit the rock he'd always been and devoted to his wife of thirty-nine years, had opted to move in with her, leaving the farmhouse empty. Tyler's sister attended med school at nearby UVA but was too wrapped up in her studies to stick around for long. The last time he'd seen her was when she'd popped by to help him move back home.

It didn't feel like home anymore. He felt unsettled, haunted by the ever-present question of *What am I going to do now?* As far back as junior high school, he'd been certain of his career path in the military. Not once had he considered that he wouldn't make it as a Navy SEAL, let alone ever asked himself what he would do if he weren't a SEAL.

When he closed his eyes, he still lived in Virginia Beach, in a condo on the oceanfront. He was still T-Rex, leader of the premier platoon in SEAL Team 12. Well, Echo Platoon was pretty sharp, too. But Charlie Platoon was strongest, in Tyler's opinion, because his men loved their jobs. They loved training for missions, honing their skills, driving themselves to the next level. They loved executing operations, arriving by air or sea like monsters out of the abyss to wipe out a present threat. They loved seizing intelligence or hostages or illegally transported weapons; it gave them purpose. Every day, they made the world a safer place for the average American citizen.

And now his platoon was without him and he without them, all because of one fateful night in

Malaysia when the roof he'd been scuttling across had given out beneath him. He'd found out later when he'd awakened in ICU in Hong Kong that an explosion on the first floor had made the roof cave in. He'd gone with it, managing to land on the top of all the rubble. While most of him had emerged unscathed, his foot had been crushed to a pulp from the ankle down. In that one unforeseen event, his family—his band of brothers—had been snatched away.

With a groan of agony, Tyler threw himself out of the chair only to recall that he'd eschewed the temporary prosthesis this morning since it chafed his ankle. He went pitching forward, hopping like a one-legged stork to keep from plowing into the wide-screen television. After a near tumble, he regained his balance, straightened to his full height, and swore.

It still came as a shock, even four months after the incident, to see his foot missing. He shook his head, disgusted with himself and with his limitations, not to mention furious with Walter Reed Hospital for taking so damn long to get him a new prosthesis that wouldn't chafe.

What now?

Lifting his head, he sent a long, thoughtful look at the antique liquor cabinet. If he were a man of weaker character, he would drown his misery in alcohol. No one would miss the liquor. Those bottles had been meant for guests who would never come again. But the house that was always bursting at the seams with fun and laughter now stood silent.

Tyler tore his gaze from the cabinet. A SEAL was made of sterner stuff than that.

You'll always be a SEAL, man. The words of his close friend Lt. Sam Sasseville echoed in his head. He could still feel Sam's firm grip on his wrist, still see the compassion and grief welling in the Echo Platoon leader's dark green eyes.

Tyler's throat closed up as he fought the urge to bellow like a wounded bear. The unexpected jangle of the doorbell startled him into losing his balance again.

He cast around for his crutch, found it, and hobbled toward the foyer. Who could this be? Not the pastor from New Life Church, he hoped. As much as he respected the man, he didn't need him dropping by on a daily basis. A glance through the parlor windows showed a black Honda SUV in the driveway with a dog in the back. Who the hell? That was not the pastor's car.

Unlocking the door, he cracked it open. The pretty woman with chestnut hair whom he'd noticed at Food Lion yesterday stood on his doorstep looking about as comfortable as a worm in hot ashes. She sent him a forced smile that made her look suddenly familiar.

"Yes?" he prompted.

"You don't remember me, do you?" Her husky voice sounded oddly familiar and extremely nervous.

"Not really," he clipped with no patience for a guessing game.

"Katie Crowley," she said, extending a dainty-looking hand. "We went to high school together."

Katie Crowley. The name did sound familiar. He pinned the crutch under his arm in order to return her handshake when the vision of a chubby girl with glasses and braces flashed through his mind's eye.

"Oh yeah," he said, stunned despite his preoccupation that she'd transfigured into such a pretty thing. Her slim hand felt a little moist, confirming her nervousness, but not at all unpleasant to hold onto.

"I'm sorry to bother you," she said, pulling it back to gesture at the back of her SUV, "but I've got a problem. See that dog?"

"Yeah." It appeared to be some kind of shepherd mix, ugly as hell, staring at them from the interior of a crate.

"I need a temporary home for him."

He set his jaw, but she plowed on.

"See, I own a kennel and a dog school, but I don't have room for him. He's housebroken and quiet and not an ounce of trouble. If you could just watch him for ten days, I'll take him off your hands then." She sucked her full lower lip into her mouth and regarded him hopefully.

Tyler frowned at her. "How do you know I'm not a cat person and I hate dogs…of any kind?"

"Because you used to have a black lab named Sadie who followed you everywhere."

Well, hell, she had him there! Plus her cat-like eyes and that dusting of freckles across her nose made it hard for him to let her down.

"Please?" Her eyebrows, darker than her wavy hair, flexed in an earnest appeal. "I have all of his food and everything. He's really no trouble. It's just ten days," she repeated. Then she licked her upper lip in a way that made his groin tingle unexpectedly.

He cleared his throat. The setup here was so bizarre he briefly wondered if he might be hallucinating, except he'd stopped using pain meds a long time ago.

"I can't take care of a dog." His refusal came out in a defensive snarl.

"Why not?" She appeared genuinely mystified.

He displayed the crutched. *Duh!* "I can't hold a leash."

"Oh, that doesn't matter." With a toss of her head, she obliterated his excuse. "Your yard is fenced," she pointed out. "Just keep him back there with you for a while, and he won't try to leave. It's the shepherd in him." She started backing down the steps, clearly taking his silence as assent, and going to fetch the dog.

"Wait," he snapped, growing more flustered by the second that this woman was ignoring him. "I never said I'd watch him for you."

"I know." She paused one step down to look up at him, her gold-green eyes as pretty as springtime. "But I really need you to, for old time's sake."

What the fuck? He barely even remembered her.

"I'll be right back. You're going to love him." And then she was jogging toward her car. His gaze fell to her bare, shapely legs, and his protest sputtered. Early May had brought in warmer weather, a circumstance for which he was suddenly very grateful.

He watched her heave open the back end of her vehicle, pop open the crate inside, and call the dog out. Tyler took one look at the silver and beige speckle-coated canine and amended his earlier opinion. The dog wasn't ugly. He was hideous—more like a dingo than a dog. Fighting the urge to back up and shut the door in Katie Crowley's face, he watched her snap a leash onto the dog's collar and lead it toward the house.

Did she not even notice he was missing a foot? "You do know that may be the ugliest dog on the planet, right?"

"I can't thank you enough," she gushed, ignoring his comment as she tugged the dog up the steps when it paused to sniff the railing. "This is Bronson. He's a blue heeler, also known as an Australian cattle dog, about a year old. His people left him at my kennel and drove off. I have no idea why they would do that. He's honest-to-God the smartest dog I've ever known."

Tyler eyed the mutt dubiously. It had finally made its way up the steps where it sat at her feet and looked up at Tyler. The heat had him panting with his mouth wide open, tongue hanging off to one side. Bright blue eyes shone out of a dark mask. His muzzle was beige, his ears perky.

"Ten days?" he heard himself say.

"Yep. One of my dogs is graduating and then I'll have room for Bronson to come back." She reached down to pat the dog's head.

"I'd better not be stuck with him," Tyler warned.

She looked back up. "Oh, you won't be."

Well, that was sincere enough. And she was so strangely appealing with her curly brown hair and cat-like eyes that he dared to ask, "Am I going to get something in return for this?"

Those same green eyes widened with surprise. "Well…I can't exactly afford to pay you," she demurred.

A wave of resentment tempered his interest in

her. "Forget it. I wasn't asking for a handout."

"Tell you what," she said, overlooking his surly reply. "I'll treat you to dinner at Tim's," she said brightly.

"Where's that?" The promise of a date occupied a spot on his utterly empty calendar.

"Oh, it's fairly new, so you don't know," she realized out loud. "It's next to the campground, right on the water." She beamed at him as she handed him the leash.

The nylon tether tempered his anticipation.

"I'll go fetch his food and crate," she offered. "Stay, Bronson." She dashed back to her vehicle, and to Tyler's surprise, the dog actually stayed, though he whined pathetically. Katie swept a big bag of food out of the back, put it on the ground, and reached for the heavy-looking wire crate.

"Damn it," Tyler muttered, watching her struggle to lower it. "Just leave it by the car," he groused. "I'll get it later."

She shot him an uncertain look. "You sure?"

So she did know about his injury even though she hadn't looked at it. "Positive."

"Okay then." With a shrug, she closed up the back of her vehicle. *Clang!* "Truth is," she said walking toward him again and rubbing her hands on her hips in a way that warmed his blood, "he'd prefer you didn't lock him up too much. Bronson doesn't like to be confined." She stopped at the bottom of the stoop to pet the dog as he strained at the leash to get near her. She stretched out a hand to pat him. "Do you, buddy?"

Then she squinted up at Tyler. "Being a shepherd, he'd prefer to case the perimeter at night. It's an instinctive thing. I'm sure you understand."

Her gold-green gaze peered deep into his soul.

"You'll be back in ten days?" he reiterated, ignoring her insinuation.

"Ten days," she promised. "Here, you can call me if there's a problem." She pulled a card from her back pocket and bounded one more time up the steps to hand it to him.

As their fingers brushed, he caught a whiff of gardenia. Glancing down, he read the card's bold lettering: **CANINE COMPANIONS**. Boarding. Training. Therapy.

"Number 4 Old Pine Road," he recited. "Where's that?" It sounded familiar.

"It's the old Roberts place where you and your friends used to drink."

He pictured the dilapidated Victorian house with its rotten floorboards and dripping spider webs and frowned. "You live there?"

"I bought it and renovated it," she explained. "Been running my business there for about five years."

"I thought the place was haunted. Didn't the previous owner murder his wife or something?"

She grimaced. "Not exactly. He was an investment banker who stole his client's money. When he went to jail, his wife hung herself on Day's Bridge."

Tyler flinched. "Damn."

"Sad story," Katie agreed. "And, yes, there's a rumor that the house is haunted. Some ghost hunters even asked if they could film a show there, but I persuaded them that they'd be wasting their time. Anyway, I can't leave my dogs for long so I need to get back." She started down the steps. "Thanks again, Tyler. I owe you."

As his gaze slid to her cut-off jeans and the legs that testified to an active lifestyle, he thought of several ways she could pay him back.

She hopped nimbly behind the wheel, started up the engine, and rolled down the window to wave. Tendrils of her chestnut hair drifted across her cheek as she turned her car around, tearing her gaze from him to look into the rearview mirror.

He and the dog stood watching until she disappeared. A whimper from the dog shook Tyler out of his trance. "She'll be back," he said, counting on it.

Basking in the warmth of her accomplishment, Katie neared her home with a dreamy smile. The wind whistling through her open window smelled of young leaves and freshly cut grass. Life was good! In all the years that she and Tyler had grown up together, she had never exchanged as many words with him as she had just then.

The encounter had left her giddy with euphoria.

He'd been terse, yes, but still polite. His grudging acceptance of the dog betrayed a strong moral character and willingness to lend a hand if he thought it was needed. Add to that his devastatingly handsome looks and she couldn't wait to see him again. Ten days was an awfully long time.

Perhaps she could take him to dinner before then. Had he taken her up on the offer? She couldn't recall. She'd been too enamored of his intense, brooding gaze and the way it affected her skin.

In ten days, Bronson would have surely won Tyler over, making it easier for Katie to say, "Oh, by the way, he's a certified therapy dog." She would have to admit it eventually and teach Tyler the commands to elicit specific behaviors. Otherwise, Bronson's hard work in learning them would go to waste.

Sunlight dappled the winding country road, brightening the shadows under the tall trees on either side and keeping her spirits lifted. But then the sun glanced off the roof of the dark car behind her, and Katie's contentment fled. It was him, her stalker—not following at a distance this time but accelerating until he rode practically on her bumper.

She tightened her grip on the steering wheel, heart thumping as he surged closer still. *My God, is he trying to hit me?* She searched the older man's pinched expression, trying to guess his intent. Suddenly, with a roar of his engine, he swung into the oncoming lane, hemming her between his oversized sedan and the narrow ditch. The deadly tree trunks flashed in her peripheral vision.

She glanced over at him as he gained on her. But with her SUV higher than his vehicle, all she could make out was the lower half of his face. He bared his teeth in a determined, ghastly grin as he edged his car ever closer.

Oh, no you don't. Katie stepped on the brakes to keep his car from bumping into hers. The Chrysler barreled past, leaving her with a clear view of its missing license plate and broken taillight. As it continued to distance itself, she eased her foot toward the gas again only to pull off the road into the nearest driveway.

A clammy sweat enveloped her. Her stalker had tried to push her off the road, or at the very least intimidate her.

With a shaky hand, she fumbled inside her purse for her cellphone and dialed her uncle's number directly.

"The intruder's not a teenager," she announced when he answered her call.

CHAPTER TWO

"LEAVE ME ALONE." Dozing in the hammock that stretched between two birch trees in his back yard, Tyler waved off the moist muzzle panting in his face. The damn dog wouldn't leave him alone. Plus, it sounded like he was chewing something he shouldn't be.

Tyler cracked an eye. A tennis ball had escaped the tennis court at the back of the yard and Bronson had found it. It dropped from his mouth and rolled into Tyler's face.

"Yuck." He sat up, annoyed, and hurled the ball across the yard. The dog took off after it, and Tyler lay back down.

The sultry afternoon made him drowsy. One of these days, he was going to have to stop being a useless, lazy son of a bitch and figure out what the hell he would do with his life. But for now, he didn't care enough to try.

He had barely closed his eyes when the ball landed on his shoulder.

"Seriously?" He glared up at the muzzle peering over the edge of the hammock. Bright blue eyes were fixed on the ball in anticipation of its being thrown again.

Tyler gripped the wet ball, thought about hiding it under his arm, and changed his mind. There was something about the dog's eyes and the playful way they sparkled that struck him as familiar. And then it came to him. Chief "Bronco" Adams, one of Tyler's closest teammates had eyes exactly like Bronson's—bluer than the sky and glinting with devilry.

"I'm going to call you Bronco," Tyler decided, pulling back his arm and giving another throw.

The dog wheeled and tore after it. *Damn, he's fast,* Tyler thought with a prick of envy.

The ball rolled into a bed of ivy climbing up the five-foot fence. The dog sniffed frantically and looked back at him. "To the right." Tyler pointed toward the ivy. Amazingly, the dog followed his directions and dove into the tangle of leaves, coming up with the ball. "Atta boy. Bring it here, Bronco."

The name felt good coming out of his mouth. It made Tyler feel like his teammates were still a part of his life. Bronco galloped proudly up to him and tossed the ball down into his lap in what nearly resembled a throw.

Tyler tossed it back testing the dog's reflexes.

Snap. Bronco caught it in his jaws and flung it immediately back at Tyler, right into his hands.

"No way," Tyler marveled. He lobbed it back at the dog, who caught it again.

"You'll never get tired this way," Tyler realized. He struggled to his foot, hopped to the tree where his crutch was propped, and moved into the yard with the ball. Then he pulled back his arm, the way he had playing quarterback for the Lions and forgetting that his follow-through required a left foot. His crutch stabbed the ground, but it couldn't halt his momentum. Down he went, shoulder first into the grass.

Ooph. He lay there for a while, humiliated and confounded by the extent of his handicap. Losing his foot had utterly wrecked his life. A single sob escaped him before he wrestled his self-pity under a lid of self-discipline.

Bronco had trotted back with the ball, but instead of dropping it on Tyler's head and compounding his defeat, the dog lay down beside him, touching the length of Tyler's side and heaving a great big sigh.

Tyler reached back absently to pat the dog's head. The position wasn't very comfortable, so he squirmed onto his other side to stroke him. The fur between Bronco's ears was especially soft.

"What's the matter, buddy?" he murmured, his

thoughts a mile away. "You think I can't throw a ball anymore? Think I'm a useless cripple, huh?"

The dog licked his wrist as if to deny the allegation, and the SEAL motto, *The Only Easy Day Was Yesterday*, flashed through Tyler's head.

"You're right. I shouldn't give up." He reached for the ball between Bronco's front paws, and the dog sprang up, eager to resume their game.

Tyler rolled to his knees. "Who needs feet?" he muttered. Staying on his knees, he hurled the ball clear to the fence with Bronco streaking along in its wake like a comet.

Katie's eyelids sprang open. The sound that had wakened her wasn't one that she heard very often. Her pregnant golden doodle, Goldie, growled low in her throat. Not only that, but the dogs in the kennel at the back of her house emitted strident punctuations of sound reserved to announce a threat. Katie had been working with dogs long enough to distinguish between the sounds they made.

Something or someone had whipped her dogs into a frenzy.

She craned her neck, peering through the shadows at the digital clock by the bed. It was 2 AM. The cause for the ruckus might just be a lost hunting dog, drawn in by the scent of other dogs to her property. That had happened before, but it was usually in the fall during hunting season, not in early

May, and rarely at night when dogs tended to bed down, even when lost.

A more sinister explanation lodged uncomfortably in her mind, causing adrenaline to flood her arteries. Katie sat up slowly, swinging her feet to the floor and reaching for the cell phone charging on her nightstand. Then she groped inside the drawer pulling out the pepper spray she'd kept close at hand since the attack in college.

The memory of the man's ugly grimace when he tried running her off the road yesterday kept her heart thudding erratically. What if it was him out there, and he tried to break in again?

Why do these things only happen to me? she asked herself. First the episode in college and now this.

At least her uncle had taken yesterday's incident semi-seriously. "Do you know any reason why anyone would want to hurt you? Have you upset any of your clients lately?" He hadn't bothered to ask if some jilted lover felt the need to harass her. It wasn't any secret that Katie didn't date.

But he hadn't believed that the road incident was in any way related to the attempted break-in.

"We caught that boy who's been stealin' jewelry out of people's houses, so you won't have any more break-ins, I can almost guarantee you. You know, this ain't the city, Katie. What happened to you back in college won't happen out here. Besides, you got your dogs to protect you."

Katie had ended that conversation mortified and discouraged. Of course her parents would have told her uncle about the incident in college. And now he probably thought her paranoid, an opinion that would only be confirmed if she called him now and the intruder turned out to have four legs, and not two.

"Come on, girl," she whispered, gesturing for Goldie to accompany her out of her bedroom onto the dark second-story landing.

The motion-sensor floodlight mounted to the kennels out back beamed brightly through her many window panes downstairs, casting geometric patterns on her furniture and walls. But all seemed undisturbed inside her house.

Holding Goldie's collar, Katie descended one step, then another. She was halfway down the stairs when the silhouette of a man's head and shoulders filled the glass pane inset into her door. With a gasp, Katie started to retreat. Someone was standing on her porch!

But Goldie had spotted him, too. Tearing free of Katie's grasp, she thundered down the stairs, rushing toward the door with a rumbling in her throat that intensified to a barrage of barking. The intruder's silhouette abruptly disappeared.

Scuttling back up to the landing, Katie dialed her

uncle's number with hands that quaked. As his phone rang in her ear, she turned her senses to Goldie's pacing. With a rash of angry barks, the retriever-poodle mix planted her front paws on the window seat built into the bay window in the parlor.

"Uncle Bill, he's back," she whispered when her uncle finally answered.

"Who's back?" he asked, clearly resurfacing from sleep.

"The intruder who was here the other day. A man just looked through the glass in my front door, the same pane that was shattered last time." A shiver coursed her spine.

"Did you see him?" He sounded more awake now.

"Yes. Well, I saw his shadow."

"I can hear your dogs barking," he noted. "Hang tight. I'll be right over."

The phone went dead in Katie's ear. She kept it firmly in one hand, the pepper spray in the other. A clammy sweat enveloped her, compounded by the first hint of summer humidity and the fact that she'd yet to turn on her air-conditioning.

Goldie ceased to bark, and the ruckus from the kennel was also dying down. Encouraged, Katie started creeping down the stairs. Maybe the intruder had caught sight of her and fled. Down the stairs she crept without anything happening to discourage her.

She was just stepping off the last step onto the varnished hardwood of her foyer when the floodlight on the kennel gate went out. Her adrenaline spiked. But the light going out was a good thing. It meant the intruder was likely gone, right?

Still the darkness ambushed her along with the memory of waking from her sleep to a stranger slicing the soft skin of her neck with his knife. Terror overwhelmed Katie suddenly, causing her knees to fold. She collapsed by the wall in a protective ball battling the fear that it would happen all over again.

Am I always going to be a victim?

Goldie padded over, panted in her ear, then curled beside her, dropping her head in Katie's lap as she'd been trained to do. Katie hugged the service dog and focused on breathing. The episode would eventually pass. Since Goldie first came into her life, episodes like this were rare. That this one had had happened at all made her furious. How dare the intruder reawaken her nightmares when she'd finally moved past them?

Tyler paced the rooms and hallways of his childhood home the same way he had paced the perimeter of the temporary camp near the Pensiangan in Malaysia. The remote village had provided a hideout for the notorious arms dealer Haji Telemong, a virtual ghost had who funneled weapons from North Korea to Al Qaida.

Tyler hadn't been able to sleep that night, any more than he could now. The hours prior to a precision attack never failed to arouse his adrenals, making sleep impossible. The whine of mosquitos and the chirping of tree frogs had kept him company as he'd contemplated the mission ahead. The perfume of frangipani flowers haunted him still, as did the taste of dread sitting on his tongue.

Untold hours of contingency planning and drilling had gone into preparing the SEALs for that strike. He should not have been so nervous. But doubts percolated—no doubt because Haji was purported to have more spies than even Hitler had, and Tyler was responsible for the welfare of fifteen men. If Haji had caught wind of their strike, who knew what could happen?

The prospect of losing any one of his men had filled him with dread. Hence, he had opted to be the first man across the roof to the entry point. Except he'd never even made it close to the window leading to Haji's private quarters before the building imploded.

The accident had resulted in the task units' emergency extraction form Pensiangan. With a shake of his head, Tyler cast off the painful memory of his recuperation and glared out of his parents' living room window. Echo Platoon was headed to

Malaysia any day now to finish what Charlie Platoon had failed to do. Sam had promised to avenge Tyler's injury personally.

More than anything in the world, Tyler wished he could join Sam. Instead, he was stuck here. His parents' overgrown lawn stretched to the white picket fence which ran along a country road. Unlike Pensingan, Louisa was a relatively safe, all-American town. Domestic violence and the occasional meth lab posed the biggest problems, along with teen vandalism. The rolling fields and forests were home to farmers and commuters who drove to neighboring cities for work but liked to get away at the end of the day.

Fireflies flickered here and there like tiny beacons of hope. But hope refused to flare in Tyler's breast. From his present vantage, the future looked as bleak and dark as the night he'd lost his foot.

If only he'd died that night. Then he wouldn't be so miserable now.

Grief swelled in his throat, making it hard to swallow. The psychologist he'd been seeing at Walter Reed had advised him not to suppress it. *Let it out,* he'd said. He'd told Tyler to picture his devastation flying out of him like a winged black beast. He willed himself to do just that. The pain tripled, but his eyes remained bone-dry.

"Fuck," he whispered. Suddenly, he was so tired

that he turned and sprawled face-down on the sofa where his mother's garden club ladies used to perch like birds on a telephone wire.

"Mama." He gazed across the dark luster of the coffee table at the pink wing-back chair reserved for the club president. It faced him, empty and ugly without her smiling presence.

The furtive approach of an interloper made Tyler tense and jerk his attention toward the door. The pointy-eared silhouette of the dog he'd taken on sucked the anxiety right out of him.

"Go away," he groaned. The dog had become his shadow, never more than a couple of yards away, regarding him with those steady blue eyes that looked more human than dog-like.

As usual, Bronco ignored him. He padded closer and whined.

"Go back to sleep," Tyler said. The dog had cried in his crate until Tyler had made him a nest by his bed.

Bronco ignored him. He lay down right next to the couch, within petting distance of Tyler's hand. Tyler found his fingers in the dog's soft fur. Bronco's rumble of contentment brought a ghost of a smile to Tyler's face. He thought about the woman who'd brought the dog over and whether she might let him pet her, too.

Whoa. Where had that thought come from?

Curiosity had made him look her up in his old year book. He hadn't realized it at the time, but even at sixteen, Katie Crowley had the makings of a beautiful woman. Plump cheeks, wild hair, and railroad tracks on her teeth hadn't disguised her potential, at least not to a mature eye. She'd made friends with the school nerds, and while intelligence wasn't an attribute he'd valued in girls back then, it sure was now.

A hankering to see her face again niggled inside him. Hadn't she promised him a date? Why should he wait for his ten days of dog-sitting to be over before he got his reward? Hell, he needed all the distractions he could get, and he was curious to see what she'd done with the old Roberts house.

Tomorrow, he decided, *I'll just drop by.*

By the time the blue lights of her uncle's cruiser dappled Katie's walls, she had regained sufficient composure to answer the door and flick on the porch light. From now on, she wouldn't forget to keep the porch light on at night.

"You all right?" he asked her with a searching look.

"Yeah."

She told him what had happened. Then he searched outside while Katie paced her wrap-around porch watching his flashlight strafe the exterior of her home. If he didn't find anything, he might tell her that her fears were unfounded. Maybe her house *was* haunted. In a way, she would prefer that to his confirming that her fears were real?

"Found some footprints in your flower bed," he announced, mounting the porch to stand beside her.

Katie swallowed hard. Relief vied with terror.

"Why don't I come in so I can ask you some questions?"

"Sure," she said leading the way inside.

They sat at her dinette table in her cozy kitchen where he asked about her past and whether anyone might have a reason to stalk her.

Katie shook her head no.

"What about the man who attacked you in college? Whatever happened to him?"

An icepick of fear pierced her heart. "He served three years in jail," she answered. "Why…why would he come after me now after all these years?"

"I'm not sayin' it's him," her uncle soothed. "Just researching my options. What ever happened with those ghost hunters who wanted to film a show here?"

"I told them they'd be wasting their time."

"And they haven't bugged you about it since?"

She shook her head, wondering if he were on to something. "No."

He tapped his fingertips on her tabletop. "Would you like me to track down your folks for you, hon?

You look pretty shaken up."

"No!" She threw both hands up. "No way. I'm not going to ruin their vacation." Her hardworking parents had been saving up for their world cruise for as long as she could remember.

Her uncle grimaced and pushed his chair back. "All right then, we'll handle this ourselves. You feel free to call me any time."

"Thank you, Uncle Bill."

She trailed him to the door on leaden feet. A real-live stalker was definitely worse than having ghosts. It was going to take all of her coping skills and the help of her therapy dog to keep PTSD from wrecking her life again.

CHAPTER THREE

THE NEXT MORNING, Tyler put Bronco in the back of his new Crown Victoria. A fresh spring scent wafted in the air, sharpening his senses that were dulled from sleep deprivation. Driving with his one good foot, he negotiated the winding country roads en route to Number 4 Old Pine Road, anticipation beating back his dark mood.

Driving made him miss his old Mustang with its supercharged V8 engine, but the clutch had necessitated a left foot, and now he didn't have one. He'd traded in the Mustang for this more subdued looking car. He resented the hell out of having to drive a tame-looking automatic, but he had to admit, the Vic was roomier and made for a smoother ride. Bronco had plenty of room in the back, looking out first one window then another, tail wagging as if to say, "Where are we goin', huh?"

Four minutes later, Tyler slowed at the black and white sign that read CANINE COMPANIONs.

Boarding. Training. Therapy. He coasted into the driveway recalling how he and his friends had haunted this place back in high school. A swarm of butterflies launched inexplicably inside him.

Approaching women had never aroused nervousness in him before. But then he'd been a popular jock in high school, and then an elite Navy SEAL. Now he was just an ordinary man—and a cripple at that. Katie Crowley was the first woman he'd attempted to approach since he'd lost his foot. What if she rejected him? His spirits sank at the distinct possibility.

A thick layer of gravel smoothed the once-pocked dirt track to the abandoned house. Sunlight danced on Tyler's windshield as he drove through the copse of pines toward the house, now visible through the tree branches.

Wow. He blinked in surprise. What had once been a gray husk of a house on a sheltered cove of Lake Anna had been transformed into a gleaming Victorian with a brand new tin roof. A coat of blue paint, white trim and lattice work, large glinting windows, and a wrap-around porch graced by a bench swing testified to its loving restoration.

"Nice," he breathed, impressed with Katie's accomplishment.

The white barnlike building behind the house wrested his attention to the kennel she'd made reference to. A sturdy chain-link fence jutted out on one side to form a sizeable outdoor holding pen. Several dogs in individual cages heralded his arrival. A couple of young black labs, a shepherd, and some breed he didn't recognize announce his arrival as he braked to a stop.

He stepped gingerly out of the car on the prosthesis that hurt his ankle, and let Bronco out of the back, keeping him on a short leash.

The dogs quieted at his approach. Tails wagging, they circled their pens and pressed their noses to the chain-link, eager to greet the dog they most certainly recognized.

Tyler entered the building proper and found himself in a bright receiving room where the sound of Katie's voice doubled his heart rate. Bronco pulled him through the open door at the back and into a hallway with the kennels on one side and some sort of training room at the other.

Katie's voice came from the training room, but Bronco was tugging Tyler toward the dogs who'd burst through the doggie doors of their individual pens into the indoor portion of their runs. As they waged their tails, whined and postured to Bronco, Tyler looked at the remaining empty pens and frowned.

Katie had told him her kennel was full. That was the reason she'd needed him to dog-sit, right? So where were all the dogs now? In the room with her?

Tying Bronco's leash to a pen so he could socialize, Tyler drifted toward the training room where he could hear Katie giving instructions. Through the cracked door, he spotted a teenaged boy in a wheel chair. The boy's mother hovered behind him, and a single yellow lab stood at the end of a leash by his side.

"Always pair the command with the gesture," Katie was saying, "and that way she'll respond to either a verbal or visual cue."

"Pick it up," said the youth with a plucking gesture.

The lab pounced eagerly at the red handkerchief lying on the ground. She snatched it up and offered it to the youth, but then she didn't want to let go.

"Sheena, drop it," Katie commanded with an air of authority that made Tyler's eyebrows rise.

The dog deposited the moist cloth reluctantly on the boy's lap.

"She's still very much a puppy, as you can see," Katie apologized with a fond smile and a treat for the dog. "But that's a good thing. She'll give you ten to eleven years of quality living."

A sudden thought stabbed Tyler's consciousness. *Quality living.* The sign at the head of Katie's driveway flashed across his mind's eye. *Boarding. Training. Therapy Certification.* He looked over at Bronco, who looked back at him as if sensing the sudden shift in Tyler's mood.

Wait one damn minute. What if Katie hadn't asked him to dog sit as a favor to her? What if she'd tricked him into a taking a therapy dog because she figured he needed help?

The appalling thought had him reassessing her from the shadows of the hallway.

Caught up in her instruction, she had yet to notice him. Everything about her appearance from the hip-hugging jeans that accentuated her athleticism to the plaid shirt that strained across her breasts appealed to him. His body responded like a red-blooded, testosterone-driven male who'd gone without sex for almost five months. But his pride bristled at the certainty that she'd lied to him. Worse than that, she had pitied him. That had to be the real reason behind her request that he take Bronco off her hands.

The dog was a stinking service dog for handicapped people! Tyler ground his molars together as a wave of mortification and outrage rolled through him. He must have made a sound or a gesture of some kind because just then Katie glanced toward the door and caught sight of him. "Tyler," she exclaimed.

He glowered at her, too stunned and chagrined to say anything.

"Would you excuse me for a minute?" With a forced smile, Katie left the youth and his mother and joined him in the hall, closing the door behind. Her cat-like gaze slid from where Bronco was tied to Tyler's stricken expression. "Is everything okay?" she asked him.

"You tell me." He hated the tremor in his voice. To think he'd driven over here intending to talk her into that date she'd promised him when all along she thought of him as nothing more than a cripple and a potential client for one of her dogs!

She didn't bother to continue the pretenses. "Tyler, I'm sorry, I—"

"You're kennel isn't even full. You lied to me. You tricked me into thinking I was helping you," he accused, steamrolling over her apology.

"I know," she said quietly. "If I'd told you the truth, you would never have taken him, would you?"

"Damn right. I don't need a therapy dog just because my foot's missing. There's nothing else wrong with me. I can still walk; I can still drive. I don't need a damn thing from anyone. I can do this myself!"

By the end of his tirade, her eyes reflected wariness and his face was burning hot.

"You can take care of your own damn dog," he added. And then he swung around and hobbled painfully toward the exit, where he paused ever-so-briefly to glance over at Bronco who had started to follow him, only to be halted by the leash. The dog returned his gaze expectantly.

Disgusted with himself, with life, with everything, Tyler hastened out of the building and strode as fast as his prosthesis allowed to his car. He half expected Katie to chase after him, offering abject apologies and stammering out excuses for her subterfuge. But he made it to his car without being assaulted.

Dropping behind the wheel, he swung his feet in, wincing when his prosthesis struck the door frame. He jammed the key into the ignition. When he glanced up, Katie was standing at the door of her establishment watching. It was then that he noticed the dark half-moons under her eyes and the unhealthy pallor of her face. She lifted a single hand in farewell, dignifying his rude behavior by acknowledging his departure.

His face burned anew. He nodded back, cranked the engine, and swung his car around in the narrow parking area. As he drove away, he glanced back once to see Katie bow her head and rub her eyes in a gesture of defeat.

Terrific, Katie thought, rubbing her eyes in the hopes of easing the ache behind them. Tyler Rexall had seen straight through her deception and now he hated her. His furious reaction had been heartbreaking. This was just what she didn't need right now—one more reason to lose sleep at night.

She looked up just as his brake lights disappeared from sight.

Recalling the couple waiting for her in the training room, she had no choice right now but to shake off her depression. Tonight, however she knew that she would wallow in it. With a heavy step, she reentered the kennel where Bronson cocked his head at her as if asking a question.

"It's not your fault, buddy," she assured him. Unclipping his leash, she opened an empty pen and ushered him inside it. Then she returned to the training room to continue working with her clients.

TYLER PUNCHED UP his pillow and groaned in frustration.

During Basic Underwater Demolition Training, the grueling candidate-elimination camp for wannabe SEALs, he'd gone three full days without sleep. As a SEAL proper, he'd managed to scrape by on just four hours of sleep a night. However, the last time he could recall sleeping more than two hours in a row was in the hospital when he'd been hooked up to an IV laced with pain-killer.

The lack of sleep was torturing him. The dark of night seemed to stretch on forever. And there was nothing to *do*—no time-critical missions. No known enemies. Just…meaningless nothingness that went on and on and on.

For a change, his thoughts tonight didn't revolve around the incident that had robbed him of purpose. His thoughts had fixated on the scene between him and Katie that afternoon, and his words replayed over and over again, giving him leisure to analyze every nuance of what he'd said.

I don't need a therapy dog just because my foot's missing.

Possibly true. He could still walk with a prosthesis, even though it pained him. He could still drive. He wasn't a cripple like the youth in the wheelchair.

There's nothing else wrong with me.

Really? Well, if that were true then he'd be sleeping like a baby right now, wouldn't he? He'd have moved past the tragedy that had left him physically and emotionally imbalanced, and he'd have figured out what the hell he was going to do with the rest of his life.

I don't need a damn thing from anyone. I can do this myself!

What a crock. He'd come home because he needed his family. Sure, they'd tried to be there for him. They'd taken the time to welcome him home and to feel out his state of mind. But his sister was busy with school, and his father had his hands full coping with his wife's decline. And then there was his mother, whom he needed most, who had kissed his scrapes and bruises all his life and told him he was good to go. She didn't even recognize him.

And that sucked. That sucked more than anything.

Hot tears slid from the corner of Tyler's eyes and slid toward his pillow.

You can take care of your own damn dog.

The memory of his last sentence to Katie made him wince. Never in his life had he spoken to a woman like that. His parents had raised him to be a gentleman, a role that he had taken seriously. He'd opened doors for women, showed them kindness and respect, never pushed for physical intimacy just because he could. While there'd never been any shortage of women in his life, he had still held himself aloof for one reason. He wanted a relationship born of respect, like the kind that his parents had.

Along came Katie, who'd planted a seed of interest regarding the future, and he'd ruined everything by squashing her selfless gesture. What an ass he'd made of himself. Hell, he owed her an apology.

Remorse burned in his gut, making it impossible to find sleep. Sitting up in bed, he found himself staring at the blanket on the floor where Bronco had curled up for the past two nights. Strange how quickly he'd gotten used to the dog there.

Now the house seemed emptier than ever.

Loneliness carved a hole in his aching chest. He swallowed hard, managed a shuddering indrawn breath before the dam burst unexpectedly.

A salvo of racking, awful noises issued from his throat. *I'm crying*, he realized, half relieved, half terrified to let his emotions get the better of him.

Let it go, urged the voice of his psychologist.

And so he did, one part of him chagrined to realize what he had been reduced to—a man with only one foot, with no future, no hope.

He sobbed until the tears ran from the hands covering his face, down his forearms to his elbow, until he felt like a wrung-out SEAL trainee in BUDs. And then, by degrees, his weeping subsided and he managed to fill his lungs without them convulsing. He felt better. But he still owed Katie an apology, and he doubted he would sleep until he'd put that chore behind him.

He reached for the phone by his bed. As usual, his former teammates Sam and Bronco and several others had sent him text messages meant to cheer him up. He decided to respond to them, but first he'd leave Katie a voicemail.

Looking up her number was the easy part. He'd taken it off her business card and put it into his contact list. Finding the words he needed to say while her phone rang was harder. But hell, it would be even tougher to talk to her in person, so he could do this.

"Hello?" A woman's voice answered on a note of dread.

"You weren't supposed to pick up." He said the first words to enter his head.

"Tyler." She heaved a sigh of relief, making him wonder whom she'd thought was calling. "What's up?"

He cleared his throat. "Well, I was calling to apologize for today. I thought you'd be asleep and I could leave a message, but that's kind of cowardly," he admitted.

"I wasn't sleeping. I can hang up if you want and you can call again and leave your message."

He smiled at the offer. "No that's all right. You deserve an actual apology." He took a deep breath and plunged ahead. "I was completely out of line today. I said things that weren't true, and I was disrespectful to you. I'm really sorry."

The silence that answered his apology had him counting his heartbeats.

"Actually, it's my fault, Tyler," she finally replied. "I should never have misled you about my reason for dumping a dog on you. His people did abandon him on my doorstep, but that was months ago. I've been training Bronson ever since."

"Bronco," he corrected. "He likes the name Bronco better."

"Okay." She gave a curious little laugh. "I'd like to hear the reason behind that."

"I'll share it with you," he promised, "on that date you owe me."

Another silence followed his veiled proposition. "Um, as I recall," she finally replied, "you were going to have to watch Brons—Bronco—for ten days, and then I'd take you out to dinner."

He loved that she was playing hard to get. "How about I promise to watch Bronco for as long as you want, and we go to dinner at that new restaurant tomorrow night?"

"Deal," she said. "But I'm paying."

"We'll go dutch," he countered.

"Fine," she agreed. "You can pick me up at seven."

She had no difficulty giving orders, either. He liked that, too. "Yes, ma'am."

A comfortable silence fell between them. "Why aren't you asleep?" he heard himself ask.

She made a little whimpering noise. "There's this man who's been following me. He's tried to break into my house, twice."

Alarm tightened Tyler's scalp. "Seriously? Have you told the police?"

"I have. My uncle—he's the sheriff now. He drops by every three hours to check on me."

Well, that was something, but Tyler could think

of more effective deterrents. "I guess you're pretty spooked about it," he observed.

"A little."

He found himself wanting to comfort her. "Let's talk more about this tomorrow," he suggested "I'd like to help catch this guy. Can't have you losing your beauty sleep."

Katie snorted. "Implying that I need it?"

"Not at all. Even with bags under your eyes, you look good."

"That's what you call a back-handed compliment."

"You want compliments? I can think of several."

"No, I'm not fishing. I'm just flattered that you're talking to me—considering I lied to you."

"But you did it for good reason," he admitted.

"Thank you," she said simply.

"I'll see you tomorrow night. Casual dress?"

"Completely casual. Good night, T-Rex."

"Good night, Katie Cat." He came up with the nickname on the spot.

He waited for her to hang up first, and then he severed the call with a warmth that spread to his extremities. Their repartee on the phone had been wonderful and unexpected. Suddenly, he couldn't wait for the hours to melt away between then and tomorrow evening when he got to take her out to dinner.

With a smile on his face, he texted back his buddies, letting them each know that he was doing okay and missing them. He finally put his phone away and lay back against his pillow. Closing his eyes, he pictured Katie as she'd looked the day she'd first come to his house. Her intelligent and insightful gaze was as sexy as her perfect curves. *Lucky me,* he thought.

The next time he opened his eyes the sun was shining and the morning was half gone.

CHAPTER FOUR

KATIE KNEW WHEN Goldie perked her ears and shot out of her bedroom that Tyler had arrived to pick her up for their outing—not technically a date since they were going dutch. She cast a critical glance into the mirror.

Too casual? She'd opted for jeans and a cream-colored top with crocheted sleeves and a demure neckline. The scar at the base of her neck was clearly visible but Katie didn't care. She found she wanted Tyler to know about what had happened to her and how she'd overcome it. The pink in her cheeks had nothing to do with the light layer of makeup she'd applied. She was looking forward to their evening together.

Don't get your hopes up, she warned herself.

Toeing on a pair of strappy sandals, she hurried down the stairs to greet him. The silhouette looming at the window pane gave her a momentary start. But then she recognized the breadth of Tyler's shoulders and her pulse leaped for a different reason. She took a deep breath, let it out again, then opened the door with what she hoped was a pleasant smile and not a cheese-eating grin.

"Hi," she said.

His golden brown eyes hit her like a gale-force wind, rocking her back on her feet as they trekked intently downward, snagging briefly on her scar. "Hi, yourself," he said looking back into her eyes.

"You shaved," she remarked, amazed at how much younger he looked without the scraggly beard.

Goldie stuck her head through the door just then, saving him from having to explain himself. "Who's this?" he asked, reaching out a hand for the dog to sniff.

"This is Goldie. She's my service dog."

His gaze jumped up questioningly, but Katie didn't elaborate.

"She's expecting puppies in a few weeks. The father is that chocolate labra-doodle in my kennels. I think they'll have beautiful pups."

Tyler stroked Goldie's soft head. "I wondered what that dog was. What are you going to do with the puppies?"

"I'll give away some and keep the two most trainable ones."

He eyed her with a growing smile. "That sounds fun."

"It is. But it's hard work, too."

A crackle of awareness passed between them as they stared into each other's eyes. "Well," said Katie, breaking the spell. "The restaurant fills up fast after seven, so we'd better get going."

He looked a bit surprised by her eagerness to leave. "Okay. You ready?"

"Let me just grab my purse." Backtracking to the closet door, she fished out her purse. "Stay, Goldie," she said, stepping outside and locking the door behind her.

Tyler was staring across the yard at Bronco, visible in the outdoor portion of his kennel. The dog yipped and made a growly sound as if trying to communicate. "I'll come back for you, buddy," Tyler called.

Katie flipped on the porch light so it would be shining when she got back. With a smile for Tyler, she let him escort her off the porch.

He limped with each step, his mouth crimped with pain, but the frown on his face told her not to comment. And once they were situated in his car, he became the competent and confident man she'd known. He shot her a smile that reminded her of how he'd looked back in high school.

"You look fantastic," he told her unexpectedly.

The gruff timber in his voice brought heat flooding to her face. "So do you." He wore a royal blue short-sleeved shirt over a pair of jeans, an ensemble that disguised his gauntness.

He said nothing for a moment, turning left at the head of her driveway and accelerating. "You're going to have to tell me where this place is," he reminded her. "I'm just driving all distracted over here."

The subtle flirtation put a bubble of happiness in her chest. "You're headed the right way," she replied. "Turn north on the 522, and it's just past the campground at the second bridge."

"Easy enough." He snapped on the radio, filling the car with the liquid voice of country-music singer Blake Shelton. A dozen questions vied for articulation in Katie's mind, but she knew the time wasn't right to ask them. If this was Tyler's first real outing since his injury—and something told her that it was—she needed to take things slowly.

They arrived at Tim's in exactly five minutes. The large, airy restaurant had been built on a finger of Lake Anna, with a deck and several windows overlooking the water. The distinct aroma of fried seafood greeted their nostrils. The hostess led them to a table for two in the corner of the room.

Too romantic? Katie wondered, grateful for the privacy, nonetheless.

Tyler pulled out a chair for her and she sank into it gracefully, lifting her bottom so he could push it closer.

Then he collapsed into the chair across from her, grimacing as he took the weight off his legs. Katie couldn't contain herself any longer. "That prosthesis really bothers you," she observed.

He shot her a fulminating look but she could tell his anger wasn't directed at her. "It sucks," he bit out. "They're making me another one."

"Who's they?"

"The amputee clinic at Walter Reed."

She winced. "That's a horrible word," she admitted not needing to repeat it in order for him to understand.

"Yes, it is," he agreed. He snatched up his menu and pretended to study it.

"The fish here is good," she said helpfully. "So are the crab cakes."

The waitress came with their drinks. Katie had ordered a glass of white wine, while Tyler stuck to iced tea.

"You don't drink?" Katie asked. In high school, he'd been known to put away a six-pack all by himself.

"Afraid if I start, I won't stop," he drawled without looking up from his menu.

Sensing the tension thrumming in him, Katie cast about for something to say that would put him at ease. Why not admit to her high school crush? It might go a long way to soothing his battered pride.

"I had a serious crush on you in high school, you know," she confessed.

He looked up, startled. A flicker of interest lit his eyes. "This is where I lose points for barely remembering you," he admitted on a rueful note.

She waved his apology aside. "Trust me, I was entirely unmemorable."

He set his menu aside. "Or maybe I was just blind," he suggested.

A blush heated Katie's cheeks and she hid it by pretending to study the menu.

A waiter sidled up to their table. They both ended up ordering identical plates—stuffed flounder with a salad and hushpuppies on the side.

"So tell me what you did after high school," Tyler requested.

Her chest tightened. *Here goes.* "I went to UVA to study psychology."

He kept quiet, seemingly quite interested.

"However, my junior year, a local man climbed through my dorm window and attacked me at knife point."

Tyler's expression darkened. His gaze dropped to the scar on her neck.

"I was saved by another student pounding on my door, but…" She drew a shaky breath. It was still so difficult to talk about. "The episode pretty much shattered my sense of safety. It took a year just to step out of my house and several more years of therapy to live a productive life again. My parents got me Goldie, and that's when I got my life back. I finished my degree online and decided to train my own service dogs."

"Including Bronco," he inserted. He seemed intrigued by the notion of her getting her life back.

"Yes. He's the smartest pup I've ever come across."

Tyler nodded. "I noticed that."

"What made you change his name?" she asked, relieved to shift the focus elsewhere.

"I'll show you," he decided, pulling out his cell phone. She watched him thumb the screen before handing it across the table.

The phone displayed a picture of several bearded warriors, each one dressed in camouflage and bristling with weaponry. Their confident poses and bad-ass expressions were the first thing Katie noticed. She spotted Tyler by his jet-black beard. The others looked as young and robust as he did.

"You see the guy on the right with the lighter hair and blue eyes?"

"Yes."

"He's a great friend—all smiles and fun-times with a can-do attitude. The dog reminded me of him."

"They do resemble," Katie agreed taking in the

man's blue eyes and killer smile. "Though I'd have to say he's a good deal more handsome than Bronson."

"All the women say that. His name's really Brantley Adams, but everyone calls him Bronco because he used to be a champion bronco rider."

"No kidding." And now he was obviously a SEAL. "Do the others have nicknames?" She held the phone sideways so he could see it, too.

"Some of them. That guy there is my peer—was my peer," he amended with a quick frown. He pointed out a swarthy-skinned godlike creature with hair as black as his, but less facial hair. "His name's Sam. I wouldn't recommend calling him anything else. Then there's Cooper, a junior lieutenant." He pointed to a lanky blond. "The young one we call Bamm-Bamm." He pointed to stockier youth who looked about nineteen years old. "The Asian guy goes by Haiku. And this is Jeremiah Winters." The last warrior was the tallest with intelligent-looking features. "His first name's Jeremiah, but we all call him Bullfrog."

"Jeremiah was a bullfrog," she quoted. Then she arched an eyebrow. "Is that supposed to be complimentary?"

"To a frogman, absolutely," he said with conviction. "Makes him the mac-daddy of us all."

His smile fled as he realized that he'd once again

included himself in their number. He gently plucked the phone from her hands and he put it away, avoiding eye contact.

"You'll always be a SEAL, Tyler," she assured him quietly.

He blinked thoughtfully, avoiding her gaze. "Funny, that's what Sam said to me. But I don't feel like one."

She longed to soothe him with further reassurances but something within her sensed he didn't want to hear empty platitudes right then. "How's your family?" she asked him.

But his expression only darkened more. "Mom's at the rehabilitation center in Gordonsville. She didn't recognize me the last time I visited."

His flat tone could not disguise his heartbreak. "I'm so sorry, Tyler. Don't stop visiting," she advised. "You never know when she'll have a lucid moment."

"Maybe you'd like to come with me next time?" he suggested, raising his gaze from the tablecloth.

"I'd love that. Does she like dogs? Seeing an animal can sharpen the mind."

He cocked his head with visible hope. "Yeah, she loves dogs."

Katie shrugged. "Okay. Just tell me when you want to go, and I'll arrange my schedule to do it."

"Who's been stalking you?" he asked out of the

blue.

The reminder of her present troubles edged aside her eager anticipation. "I have no idea." She explained how she'd arrived home one day to see a man fleeing from her front door. He'd left her dogs in an uproar and the pane set into her door shattered.

"Then I kept seeing the same maroon Chrysler in my mirror, like he was following me. He tried to push my Honda off the road the other day."

Concern hardened the line of Tyler's already chiseled jaw.

"Then the last episode happened just two nights ago. He tried to break in while I was sleeping."

"Christ," he swore. To Katie's surprise, he extended a hand across the table, palm-side up.

Katie accepted his gesture of comfort, laying her own hand atop his. The firm but gentle pressure of his fingers as they crooked around hers made her mouth turn dry.

"That must have awakened some painful memories," he deduced, rubbing his thumb across her knuckles.

"Definitely," she breathlessly agreed. "But Goldie is trained to get me through panic attacks."

He eyed her curiously, unaware of his effect on her tingling nerves. "You think Bronco will help me the same way?"

"I wouldn't have foisted him on you if I didn't think so."

He nodded and looked down at her hand. "Your skin is so soft."

"Shea butter," she replied. "Trust me, if I didn't use it day and night, my hands would be scarred and callused from hauling on leashes."

"You should be proud of the work you do," he said.

"I am."

The waiter approached them again with their food, forcing her to pull her hand back and concentrate on eating.

The meal passed in a blur of pleasant conversation. Tyler, she discovered, shared many of her interests, from music to following current affairs. Even their political views were similar. By the time they finished eating, she felt comfortable trailing him out onto the deck that overlooked the water. A cooling breeze wafted across the inlet, making the waves dance and glitter in the waning sunlight. The swallows that had built nests under the adjacent bridge dipped and whirled, reflecting the tumult in Katie's innards when Tyler caught up her hand.

Only a couple times since college had she allowed herself to get physically intimate with a man, and both relationships had ended with her calling it off. Holding hands with Tyler was heavenly. But would she balk later if intimacy became a regular affair?

"I should probably get back," she told him. Regret vied with her desire to stay in this perfect moment forever. "I don't like to leave my dogs alone for long."

He cut her a searching look. "No problem." Then he led her back to his car, and sped her safely home. For a change, they didn't speak, except to discuss the wild turkeys that hobbled across the road, forcing them to slow down.

"You don't see that every day," Tyler observed.

As he pulled into her driveway, slowing in front of her house, Katie turned her body to face him. "I had such a nice time," she assured him, both longing for and dreading a parting kiss.

He sent her a wry smile. "I'm supposed to bring Bronco home with me," he reminded her.

"Oh, that's right." They both climbed out of the car to cross the dark yard when suddenly Tyler flashed out a hand and seized her wrist.

Startled, Katie looked over to find him staring at her front door.

"I thought you left the light on," he observed.

Yes, she had, but now her porch stood in darkness. However, there was still enough light for her to see that her window pane had been shattered all over again. "No!" she cried, racing for the door.

Even with his painful prosthesis, Tyler managed to catch her elbow as she mounted the steps. "Call your uncle," he said in a calm voice that helped to dissipate her horror. "I'll go inside and check things out."

"Find Goldie," she called after him. The fear that her pregnant dog had been hurt by the intruder made her movements less than competent as she fumbled for her cell phone and dialed her uncle's number. What if the intruder had a gun? Could Tyler hold his own against him?

Waiting for her uncle to answer, Katie watched through her windows as Tyler went from room to room flipping on the lights. Her uncle's voicemail answered, and Katie left a succinct message asking him to call her right back. Suddenly, there was Tyler, stepping through her door with a broom.

"You can come in," he stated. "Goldie's okay. He bribed her with a meaty bone. But brace yourself. The intruder tore up your window seat in the parlor."

Bewildered as to why, Katie sidestepped the glass Tyler started sweeping and entered her home with a held breath.

The formal parlor had been the coup de grace of her renovation project. Expensive crown molding accented the pale yellow walls. Her furniture was a tasteful blend of modern and Victorian. A working clock from 1912 ticked over her whitewashed mantle. Nothing had been disturbed except the window seat. The cushions had been ripped off and tossed onto the floor. Someone had taken a hatchet to the wood beneath, pulling up and breaking off several planks to reveal the empty space below.

Katie clapped a hand over her mouth to stifle her dismay. If it wasn't enough that she would have to replace the window in her door a second time, now she would have to make repairs to the window seat. "What on earth?" she cried as Tyler came up behind her. "What—what was he looking for?"

"My guess is money," he suggested.

"Money?" She whirled around to look at him.

"Think about it. The former owner went to jail for embezzling his client's money. What if he hid it in this house thinking he could find it again when he got out?"

Just then her cell phone rang, and she took the call, telling her uncle what had happened, and suggesting Tyler's theory. "He'll be right over," she relayed, putting her phone away.

Tyler offered her a sympathetic hug "Better finish sweeping up," he said, turning away.

Katie found Goldie lying in the kitchen gnawing on an oversized knuckle bone.

"You don't need this," she sternly informed the dog. Tossing the bone into the trash, she threw herself down at the kitchen table until Goldie wandered over and gazed into her eyes, steadying her erratic heartbeat.

CHAPTER FIVE

TYLER SAW THE sheriff back to his car. The man had arrived in a timely-enough fashion, but then he wouldn't leave. After listening to Tyler's theory, he had called a number of individuals to gather reports on the former owner. Dale Roberts had stolen over thirty-thousand dollars of the investment money his clients had entrusted to him. Only twelve thousand of that sum had ever been recovered, making Tyler's theory a viable one.

Roberts had been convicted in 1983 and served eight years of a fifteen year sentence only to end up right back in jail for failing to report to his parole officer. Since then, he'd committed a rash of crimes that kept him incarcerated, including fraud and grand larceny. A recent phone call to the state police confirmed he'd just been paroled again in April.

"Shouldn't take us long to find him," the sheriff said, speaking out of his lowered car window as he snapped on his seatbelt. "I've got the shoe molds and a couple of good fingerprints. We'll get him on breaking and entering this time."

Tyler watched the patrol car roll away. Sensing someone's eyes on him, he looked over to find all the dogs in the kennels standing alertly in their pens. Their gazes seemed to be fixed on the porch. Tyler swung around to find Katie standing by the pile of swept glass, hugging herself. The porch light, now back on, turned her chestnut hair to amber. Drawn to her like a moth to flame, Tyler climbed the steps and searched her pallid face. Her eyes reflected lingering shock. She appeared to be trembling.

"You all right?" he asked her.

She started to nod then changed her mind and shook her head, no. It was all he could do not to reach for her and enfold her in his arms, offering the reassurance she so obviously needed. But her skittishness earlier that night and the story of what had happened to her in college kept him in check.

"Would you…like for me to stay?" he asked haltingly.

"Please," she said without the least hesitation. With that, she stepped right up to him and threw her arms around his waist. He could feel tremors running up and down her spine. He could also smell a delicious hint of gardenia, dryer sheets, and woman. My God, how long had it been since he'd inhaled that subtle and arousing scent?

It took every ounce of discipline to return her embrace without openly caressing her. She wouldn't welcome his advances—not tonight, maybe not ever.

"Okay," she said, stepping back and visibly collecting herself. "Why don't we watch a movie? I doubt I could sleep right now."

The movie turned out to be an action adventure flick. By the time it was over, the night's fright had retreated and Katie declared herself ready to go to bed.

"I have a guest room," she said, canceling out his stubborn little hope that she would ask him to sleep with her.

"I guess Bronco's okay in the kennel?" he asked, thinking he might at least get to sleep with the dog.

"I'll bring him in if you like."

"Sure, if it's not too much trouble."

"Not at all."

He trailed her outside, taking the opportunity to reconnoiter the yard and make certain the intruder wasn't still lurking about. But lightning bugs and cicadas were all that he saw and heard.

Bronco greeted him with enthusiasm, flanking his side as he followed Katie back into the house. She led them to a room on the second level, immediately adjacent to what he guessed was the master suite.

"Nice," he said taking in the contemporary décor and café-au-lait colored walls. Bronco found a braided rug on the floor, circled it twice and lay down.

"The bathroom is right across the hall," she said, pointing it out. "Do you need anything else?"

Just you, he thought, surprised by how quickly his attraction for her had heated to full-blown desire. "No, I'm good."

"All right. Well, if you change your mind, I'm right next door. You might hear me get up at night. I'm not the best sleeper."

"Me neither." He grimaced at the understatement.

"Goodnight." Sending him a shy smile, she turned away, calling for Goldie to join her in her bedroom, and closing the door behind her.

Tyler reconnoitered the room, inspecting knick-knacks and framed photographs, including one of her smiling parents. She had told him tonight that they were on a world cruise. The queen-sized bed looked inviting with its downy white comforter. He went across the hall and prepared for bed, brushing his teeth with a finger. Then he returned to the room, freed his aching stump from the hated prosthesis, and slipped into bed.

Snapping off the light, he pricked his ears over Bronco's steady breathing to the silence coming from the other room. If Katie wasn't sleeping, she was sure being quiet. He closed his eyes and willed himself to sleep, but his body thrummed with awareness. He was still too-keyed up to lose consciousness. An hour passed, then another. He rolled over and groaned into his pillow. Why were nights so impossibly endless?

Suddenly he heard Katie's doorknob turn. Stealthy footfalls sounded outside of the guestroom door, which he'd left intentionally cracked. Her approach had him holding his breath and wondering what she wanted.

"Tyler?" She whispered his name so quietly that if he were sleeping—and anyone other than a trained SEAL—it wouldn't have awakened him.

He sat up abruptly as she pushed his door farther open, and Bronco did likewise.

"Are you awake?" she asked earnestly.

"I think so," he said with a smile.

She just stood there, dressed in a short teddy that made his pulse accelerate and his internal temperature rise.

"Everything okay?" he asked.

"I can't sleep," she admitted, hands fisted at her sides.

Welcome to my world, he thought.

"I was thinking—" She cut herself off.

"That maybe you'd sleep better over here?" he

suggested, praying he was right.

"Exactly. I mean, just...*sleep* in the same bed."

No way was he going to sleep a wink with her shapely body lying next to his. "Sure," he said, tossing back the covers and scooting over to make room for her.

"Thank you." With a pat on the head for Bronco, she wriggled into the space he'd made, sighing with relief then turned onto her side to gaze at him in the dark. He could just make out the whites of her eyes and the curve of her nose by the moonlight slipping through the window sheers. "Goodnight," she said, closing her eyes.

"'Night." He lay flat on his back, fighting the awareness of her proximity as it clawed at him. He'd never been more painfully conscious of his missing foot. Did it make him any less of a man in her eyes?

Minute by agonizing minute, the night ticked by. The dog started snoring. Tyler's long-neglected manhood throbbed with the need to be stroked. But that was wishful thinking.

Suddenly, Katie squirmed closer, rolled into his body and threw a leg over his. Tyler froze, the breath wedged in his lungs, his heart thudding. Did she even know what she was doing? Her foot was touching his appended ankle. He was afraid to speak, to wake her up if she was sleeping. Besides, he could feel the weight of one full breast resting on his chest and it felt exquisite.

"Do you think I could have a tiny kiss?"

Her soft question almost stopped his heart. "Uh, sure," he said, having to pull his shoulder out from under her head in order to come up on one elbow. Her cat-like eyes caught and held the starlight. He leaned over her, only too willing to indulge in a kiss. His heart thudded in anticipation.

Ducking his head, he planted a chaste and tender kiss on her lips.

Her fingers slid into his hair, curled into it, and pulled his head down to do it again. There was nothing chaste or tender about the second kiss. She met it with a willingness to participate that curled his toes. Desire swept through him with hurricane force. He tamped it down, striving for restraint.

At last she pulled back. "That was nice," she said, sounding faintly surprised. "I don't know why but I'm not at all tense with you."

Implying that she locked up around other men?

"Maybe because you knew me before?" he suggested. For himself, he'd practically forgotten about his missing foot. If she didn't seem to notice, what did it matter?

"That must be it. Do you think we could try it again?"

His stomach clenched with desire. "Sure." And then he kissed her again, concentrating on just the luscious taste and texture of her mouth, doing his best to ignore the breasts pushed against him.

Nice was not the word he would have used to describe the sultry, languorous twining of their tongues. Naughty came much closer. It was all he could do to hold himself in check.

Katie seized his wrist, drawing his hand to one of her breasts in a silent command to caress her.

Second base, Tyler thought, telling himself he'd be content to stay right here, kneading Katie's fullness through the filmy material of her teddy. He thumbed a stiffened nipple, and she broke the kiss with a gasp.

Out the corner of his eye, Tyler saw Bronco get up and slip through the open door. Apparently, they had wrecked his slumber. Either that, or they'd given him ideas and he was off to visit Goldie. How certain was Katie that the labradoodle had fathered Goldie's pups?

"I've never honestly enjoyed intimacy since that night in college," Katie admitted, recapturing Tyler's attention.

"We can stop now if you want." Disappointed, he started to draw his hand away.

"Oh, no." She pressed it back and sealed her lips over his. "Don't stop," she inserted between kisses. "I'm enjoying it immensely."

So was he. He was enjoying it so much he was

afraid she'd want to stop before he got to third base. With rising hope, he gathered the material of her teddy and lifted it up the length of her body, revealing creaming looking skin, supple muscles, and bodacious curves. "Christ, you're beautiful," he exclaimed.

To his gratification, she raised her arms and arched her back invitingly. Encouraged, Tyler stripped off his boxers, which was all he had on. She watched every move, her fascination only fanning his arousal.

"I can't believe this is happening," she purred, touching her breasts in an unconsciously erotic gesture.

"Let me do that." Tyler lowered his head to lap at a taut nipple. Her hum of pleasure had him moving to the other one. And then he moved slowly and implacably down the length of her body, worshiping her with his mouth. "You just tell me if you want me to stop."

"Please don't stop," she begged.

He felt himself smiling. He kissed her hip bones and the insides of her quivering thighs, inhaling her perfume until it left him giddy. "You smell so good," he muttered.

As he moved his mouth to the apex of her thighs, she spread them in invitation, gazing down the length of her body at him.

"That's beautiful," she said on a note of wonder. A second later her head fell back in delight. "Oh, Tyler."

She will not regret this, Tyler vowed. He devoted himself to the mission at hand—to bring her more pleasure than she'd ever known in her life. He lavished her with all the skill he could muster, listening to her ragged breathing to determine what pleased her most.

Goosebumps played tag up the backs of her thighs. She trembled and moaned. Tyler slid a finger into her slippery heat.

"Yes," she cried, sounding at the verge of orgasm.

He added a second digit, preparing her for what was to come.

"Oh!" She lifted her hips, driving his fingers deeper.

He could feel her convulsing, feel the rush of moisture coating him. He pushed to his knees reaching for his condom in the wallet beside the bed. He had a little trouble balancing on the mattress with only one foot to brace him, but he didn't topple over.

With reawakening confidence and certainty that she wouldn't put a halt to things now, he stretched himself over her, centering his sex between her thighs. As she pulled his head down for a kiss, he sank into her with a groan of ecstasy. Her body welcomed him. Christ, it had been so long since he'd lost himself in a woman's softness. Katie's tender embrace and the way her body moved with his felt like home.

He wanted to wallow in the sweetness of the moment, to retreat and then surge into her again and again like waves rolling onto shore. However, it wasn't long before rapture overwhelmed him and he gave into it, groaning with ultimate surcease as he buried his face against Katie's neck.

Oh, man. That was…amazing.

When he'd caught his breath, he raised his head to look down at her. She returned his gaze with a dreamy-looking smile. "How was that?" he asked.

"Perfect," she replied.

He had to agree. It had been surprisingly, overwhelmingly perfect. In fact, he found himself looking forward to doing it again.

"Now I think I can sleep," she said, dashing that prospect.

He dropped a quick kiss on her lips. "Be right back," he said, experiencing his first awkward moment as he hopped naked across the room and out into the hall to discard the condom and wash up.

By the time he rejoined Katie, her rhythmic breathing told him she'd already fallen asleep. He got carefully back into the bed, willed his half-aroused member to subside, and closed his eyes. Within seconds, he was snoring.

CHAPTER SIX

KATIE BROWSED THE aisle of bird feeders at the hardware store with a smile of contentment. It had been a week since she and Tyler had first shared a bed together and, since then, a night hadn't gone by that he wasn't next to her. They both slept like rocks after indulging in highly satisfying lovemaking.

I'm in deep, she admitted to herself. Yet the acknowledgement didn't fill her with panic because she suspected that Tyler felt the same way about her. He hadn't said as much but he'd gone from morose-ly depressed to smiling and optimistic in the course of seven days.

Their trip to Gordonsville to visit his parents had helped with that, too. While Tyler's mother Lauren hadn't fully recognized her son, she'd perked up at the sight of Bronco, whom Tyler had brought along for the visit.

"Who's this?" she'd asked, stretching out a manicured hand to stroke the dog.

Barely sixty-five years old and still beautiful, Lauren Rexall radiated with a warmth and kindness that Bronco seemed to recognize at once. Katie fully understood Tyler's heartbreak over his mother's dementia.

"This is Bronco, Mama," he'd replied. "He's my service dog."

She'd looked up at him, clearly perplexed that he had called her Mama. "Why do you need a service dog, young man?" she'd asked.

A spasm of pain had crossed Tyler's face. "I lost my foot in an operation overseas. Bronco fetches things for me so I don't have to get them myself."

"Well, isn't that nice," she remarked. "You were a soldier?" she asked.

"I was a SEAL, Mama. But I can't be one anymore."

His words were clearly a call for comfort. His father had stretched out a hand and squeezed his knees.

His mother studied him as if trying to place him. "Well, whenever you get hurt, you just get back up, brush yourself off, and keep on going."

This must have been something she'd said to him in the past because tears welled into Tyler's eyes, and it was all he could do to contain them.

But a wound inside him had healed during that

visit. And now Katie was looking for the perfect bird-feeder to place outside his mother's sitting room window so she had something to look at. She selected one with a pole that Tyler could drive into the ground and a gismo on the pole to confound squirrels. Paying for her purchase at the register, she made her way back to her car.

The dark cumulus clouds piling up on the horizon promised an afternoon thunderstorm that would bring in a cool front. Katie had just laid her purchases in her trunk when she sensed someone coming up behind her. She turned just as a stranger seized her arm in a cruel grip. The cold gray eyes of a man in his sixties bore into hers. In his other hand, he held a knife, the blade of which threatened to gouge her abdomen.

"Where is it?" he snarled, assaulting her with foul breath. "Where's the money you took from me?"

This had to be Dale Roberts, her stalker. "I don't have your money," she protested, speaking through stiff lips as the shock of being held at knifepoint registered.

"Where is it?" he snarled.

"I have no idea. Someone probably found it before I bought the house. It wasn't there when I renovated. Please, leave me alone," she dared to add. "You've done enough damage."

His grip only tightened. "Oh, I don't think so.

You took my money and I expect it back. Get in the car," he exhorted, hauling her toward the passenger seat and stuffing her in it.

For a moment Katie thought he meant to drive her car, but then he told her to climb through to the driver's seat. Taking her place, he shut them both in.

"Drive!" he added, threatening her with the knife.

"Where—where are we going?" Katie stammered, fumbling to insert the key she still clutched into the ignition. Then she backed out of the parking space, her coordination impaired by fear.

"To the drive-thru at your bank. I want all the money in your accounts."

She tugged the shifter into drive and made her way to the road, scarcely aware of the other cars around her. "There's not very much in there," she protested. "It cost me three hundred dollars to replace the glass in my door, which you broke—*twice*."

"Just shut up and drive," he hissed.

Her bank stood virtually across the street. Katie lurched into the road then merged into the right lane. She was turning into the bank when she glimpsed Tyler's Crown Victoria heading in her direction in the oncoming traffic. *Tyler!*

Desperate to catch his eye, she took her foot off the gas. She could see Bronco riding in his back seat.

Tyler's gaze alighted on her Honda and his face lit up. He lifted a hand to salute her only to lower it again when he spotted the man in the car with her. Katie's heart thudded painfully as she turned into the bank's parking lot. Could Tyler guess by the look on her face what was happening?

As she guided her car under the awning into the drive-thru, a torrent of rain began to pelt the area around them.

"Hurry up," Roberts demanded.

Katie glanced down at the blade in his hand. It looked to be at least five inches long.

Scarcely able to think, she riffled through her wallet looking for her bank card and ID. Then she lowered her window and reached for the cylinder to put them inside, only to find that she hadn't pulled up closely enough. "I have to open my door to reach it," she said, looking for the man's permission.

"Back up and get closer," he ordered.

She glanced in the rear view mirror. "I can't. There's already someone behind me."

"Fine. But don't try anything stupid." He gave her impetus to obey him by sticking the point of the knife against her ribs.

Katie swallowed hard, eased her car door open, slid over to put one foot down on the ground. She seized the cylinder. It took her quaking fingers several seconds to get it open. She dropped the cards inside, put the cylinder back into the tube and sent it flying into the bank. A second later, the teller's pleasant face appeared on the video monitor welcoming her to the bank. "How can I help you today, Miss Crowley?" she asked.

"Uh, yes, I need all the money in my checking and savings," Katie told her in a shaky voice.

"All of it?" The teller looked concerned. "You're required to keep a minimum balance of two hundred in your savings."

Katie cast a pleading glance at Roberts, but his only answer was to prick her side with the tip of his blade. Katie hissed with discomfort as the point sliced into her skin. Couldn't the teller see by her stricken expression that she was acting under duress?

She didn't want give to Roberts what little she had left in her savings. But her life and her well-being mattered far more. "Then I guess I have to close my savings account," Katie answered. "I really need all of it."

The woman studied her for a troubled moment. "All right, then," the woman finally agreed. "Just a minute."

Katie's door remained cracked. Her left foot still touched the ground outside of the SUV. What if the money wasn't enough to satisfy Roberts? After all, the sum total was probably a far cry from the amount he'd hidden. Hadn't Uncle Bill said that twenty thousand dollars of the money he'd stolen had never been recovered? What if Roberts decided to abduct her in order to ransom her for the remaining balance? She had to get away before the idea crossed his mind.

A layer of cold sweat settled on her skin as she waited for just the right moment to make her move. Her pounding heart rocked her entire body. The drum of rain spattering the lot around her masked the sound of her ragged breaths. For once, she was glad that Goldie wasn't with her. With her pups due any day now, Katie hadn't wanted to risk bringing her along. Roberts didn't look like a man who loved animals.

The rumble of the cylinder in the tube was Katie's cue to act. *Get ready*. She waited for the money to drop into the slot and the plastic window to slide up. Then, shifting all of her weight onto her left foot and pretending to reach for the money, she kept right on going. In her haste, she tripped over the cement island, scraping her palms against a brick pillar as she caught herself.

The man's bellow of outrage galvanized her, flooding her with a fresh dose of adrenaline that lent her speed. She fled from her vehicle running straight into the rain and then into the air-conditioned bank, startling the employees.

"Quick!" she cried. All three of them looked at her like she'd lost her mind. "Someone call the police. The man in my car is taking all my money. He forced me at knifepoint to withdraw everything!"

A woman at the desk snatched up her phone. Katie whirled around to peer outside. The sight of Tyler's Crown Vic easing around the building brought a cry of relief to her lips.

Whoever the man was with Katie, he was now seated at the wheel and getting money in the drive-thru. Where the hell had she gone? Tyler had known instantly by the look on her face that she'd been in trouble. That certainty had tightened his chest and spurred him into action.

He slowed to a stop, scanning the area for any sign of her. Suddenly, there she was, materializing in his driver's side mirror as she dashed toward his car through the deluge. She popped open his passenger door and dove inside, her face as white as a sheet, her entire body drenched.

"Katie, what's—?"

"He's taken all my money," she relayed with gunfire urgency.

"Who?" His gaze swung automatically to her Honda as it started pulling away.

"Dale Roberts, the man who broke into my house looking for the money. He grabbed me in the parking lot across the street."

Tyler veered into the lane that was closed in order to get around the car blocking their way. Bronco staggered in the back seat. "Are you okay?" he asked, raking Katie for any sign of harm. "Did he hurt you?"

"I'm fine," she said, groping for her seatbelt. "I told the people in the bank to call the police, but I should call my uncle directly."

Tyler gripped the wheel harder. "Tell him I'm not letting this bastard out of my sight."

The bastard in question had turned right out of the parking lot and was speeding toward the intersection where the light was turning yellow. Tyler gunned his engine trying to avoid getting stopped by the red light. Fortunately, the Honda merged right, avoiding the light. Tyler chased after it. Pounding rain blurred the image of the SUV as it flew up the road before them.

"Oh," Katie exclaimed. "I don't have my phone with me. My purse is back in my car."

"Here, use mine." He teased his iPhone from his front pocket, telling her the password as he handed it to her. With one ear, he listened to Katie relay to her uncle what happened.

"We're on 208 South, chasing him now," she added, "headed toward the highway. He's going really fast."

So was Tyler. He glanced at his speedometer,

surprised to find that they were doing over seventy miles per hour on a winding, hilly road. But the downpour had eased into a light drizzle.

Roberts had to know by now that he was being followed. He continued to drive at a break-neck pace. Sheets of water sprayed from his tires as he barreled through the deepening puddles. Trees and deep ditches flashed by Tyler's peripheral vision.

It's not worth forfeiting our lives to get this guy. The realization had him easing his foot off the accelerator. It also made him realize he was looking forward to the future.

"What are you doing?" Katie asked. "He's getting away."

"He won't get far," Tyler assured her. "Your uncle will have the state police waiting by the interstate. Besides," he shot her an unguarded look of affection, "I'm not taking chances with your life."

She sent him a searching look.

"I'm falling for you, Katie Crowley. I hope you realize that."

Maybe it wasn't the right time for a love-confession, but the tremulous smile she sent him and the riot of color that banished the pallor from her cheeks made it worthwhile.

"You're falling for me?" she asked, clearly forgetting that they were caught up in the middle of a high-speed chase.

“Is there something wrong with that?” Belated uncertainty pricked him.

“Not at all,” she said with enough gusto to ease his worries. “I’m just…Well, you know I’ve always been crazy about you.”

“Don’t know what I did to deserve that,” he drawled. The situation ahead of him wrested his attention forward. “Oh, shit.” His gaze locked on the Honda as it hydroplaned across a sheet of water. The back end of the vehicle skated sideways, and suddenly the whole thing started to flip.

Katie screamed in horror as her SUV rolled three hundred and sixty degrees, slammed sidelong into a ditch and came to a crashing, shuddering halt as it struck a wall of tree trunks. Finally, it came to rest on all four tires.

Unfazed by the sudden violence—he had seen far worse—Tyler threw an arm across Katie’s chest as he slowed to a halt half a football field away. Bronco plowed into the back of the front seat. With a glance into the rearview mirror, Tyler swiftly backed his Crown Vic off the pavement and onto a utility road. “We’re okay,” he said, gripping her arm reassuringly. “Listen, there are flares in the trunk. Break them all open and place them on the road. Make sure you put one at the top of the hill.”

“Where are you going?” she cried. Bronco, in tune to her distress, whined and paced the rear seat.

"I'm going to get your money back." *And see if the man's still alive*, he added to himself.

"Be careful!" she called after him.

He started down the hill toward the accident, wincing with each step. A glance back saw Katie bent over, head inside his trunk looking for the flares. She had left her door open. Suddenly, Bronco bolted out of it, chasing after him. Tyler stopped and pointed at the car. "No," he said, "go back!"

The dog stopped on the side of the road. Katie looked up and called him.

"Just get the flares," Tyler called. "Don't worry about the dog." He turned toward the Honda again, and that was when he saw the man—white envelope in hand—pushing out of the crumpled driver's side. A scarlet stain streaked one side of the man's face, suggesting he had hit his head. With a sneer of determination, Roberts clutched the money envelope to his chest with one arm. The other, obviously broken, hung uselessly from his shoulder as he took off running, straight into the woods across from the SUV.

"Fuck," Tyler raged, going after him.

If walking in his current prosthesis was painful, then running brought exquisite agony. But he'd trained for situations just like this. He knew in his mind that he was faster—at least he used to be. Ignoring the pinching that hindered his chase, he lengthened his stride.

Roberts was an old man and injured at that. *I've got this,* Tyler thought, but the man was managing to put distance between them. Furthermore, his pea-green shirt blended with the lush foliage, making it hard for Tyler to keep him in his line of sight. At times, the sound of him crashing through the undergrowth was all that kept Tyler on course and, even then, the wail of sirens as the police arrived at the crash site muffled the man's escape.

Suddenly, a body of dark fur brushed past Tyler, startling him. Bronco, too, was giving chase, no doubt thinking this was just another game.

"Bronco!" Tyler reproached, but the dog ignored him, dodging trees with dexterity that Tyler could only envy. He huffed after the animal, breathing in the scent of pine, bark, and leafy debris. He had just crested an incline when the crashing ahead of him turned into a rash of swearwords and frightened pleas.

Hopping on one foot to give his battered left ankle a break, Tyler approached a scene that made him throw his head back and laugh—the first full-throated laugh he'd issued in months.

Bronco stood atop Dale Roberts, pinning him to the ground with his forelegs and licking his ears. The man was obviously terrified the dog was going to make a meal of him.

"Stay, Bronco," Tyler ordered, throwing up the signal Katie had taught him to use. Bronco performed the task unfailingly. Not until he was close enough to put his own shoe on the man's back did he release the dog. "Do what I say," he warned Roberts, "or my dog will tear your throat out."

The man babbled incoherently. With nothing to bind the man's wrists with, Tyler bit his fingers into pressure points on his left shoulder. "Stand up," he ordered.

Roberts groaned with pain, but he nonetheless complied, dropping the envelope stuffed with money in the process.

"Bronco, pick it up," Tyler said as he twisted the man's good arm behind his back. The other was already completely useless. The dog delivered the envelope gently into Tyler's outstretched hand, and he stuck it in his pocket. "Turn around and walk back to the road," he ordered the felon, using the voice he reserved for enemy combatants.

Returning to the road on his miserable piece-of-shit prosthesis was the hard part of bringing back the perpetrator. Fortunately, Tyler ran into Sheriff Crowley and two deputies who'd waded into the woods looking for them. They took Roberts off his hands, cuffed him and read him his rights before they tramped back to the crash site. It was all Tyler could do to keep up with them, concealing his limp and holding his head high.

The sight of Katie waiting, her anxious expression transforming into a smile of relief as she caught sight of him, beat back a portion of his agony. She rushed into the woods, hugging him and putting a shoulder under his arm. He leaned his weight on her, grateful for her keen intuition—for the hope she'd given back to him through her love and the gift of Bronco.

"Son, you did good," Sheriff Crowley said, as his deputy stuffed Roberts into a squad car. "He might well have gotten away from us if you hadn't stopped him."

"Honestly, it wasn't me," Tyler had to admit. "Bronco's the one who stopped him. He had him pinned to the ground, crying like a baby."

Bill Crowley cut the dog a considering look. "Well-behaved, too," he observed noting how Bronco had come to sit at Tyler's feet. "Say, you wouldn't be interested in working on the force, would you?"

The offer caught Tyler off guard. "Well, I've got a slight disability," he protested, wondering how the man had overlooked it.

"Aw, hell," said the man. "You can still run faster than I can with this gut." He jiggled his pot belly. "And maybe we could train your dog to be a K-9 cop, too."

"He's highly trainable," Katie inserted, lifting her eyes to gauge Tyler's response.

Tyler thought about it. Why not? Being a cop wasn't as glamorous or critical as being a SEAL, but he could still use plenty of the skills he'd worked so hard to master, and he could still protect American citizens, even if they all lived right here in his own hometown. "Thank you," he said. "I'm going to seriously consider it."

"You do that, son." The sheriff clapped him on the back.

"Oh," Tyler added, remembering the envelope in his pocket and pulling it out. "I guess you'll need this for evidence? This is the money he took."

Crowley took the envelope and quickly bagged it. "Don't worry, hon," he said to Katie. "I'll see you get every cent of it back tomorrow. Thanks for protecting my niece," he added, nodding at Tyler one more time before turning away. "Evans, call for a tow truck!" he bellowed.

Tyler followed Katie's gaze to her battered Honda Pilot.

"Sorry about your car, Katie Cat," he said, giving her a squeeze.

"That's okay," she answered glumly. "I've got insurance."

"What's your deductible?"

She heaved a heavy sigh and turned her head to

send him a wry smile. "Almost exactly what's in that envelope."

"Come on," he said, with a compassionate squeeze. "Let's get your purse and phone and take you home. I've had enough excitement for one day."

EPILOGUE

"YOU LOOK SO happy," Katie remarked, as they left the Military Advanced Training Center inside of Walter Reed National Military Medical Center and stepped into the elevator. "Does it still feel good?" She punched the button that would take them to one of the suites allotted to amputees getting treatment. They would stay there for two nights while Tyler underwent gait testing and assessment.

"It feels great," he replied on a note of wonder. She noticed he could not stop staring at his new prosthesis, clearly visible where it stuck out from his tennis shoe and connected to his ankle. "Almost feels like a real foot."

According to the prosthesis' specs, it worked almost like a real foot, too. His appended tibia fit snugly in a casing lined with soft silicone to prevent chafing. Beneath the casing, an ankle, jointed to bend just like a real one, connected to a carbon fiber pedestal that fit inside his shoe just the way a real foot would.

"I feel like I'm dating the bionic man," Katie teased.

He shot her a grin. "I wouldn't go that far. But now I can keep up with the other deputies."

Katie rolled her eyes. "You can do more than that and you know it."

Their eyes met as the elevator doors closed, and the elevator began to rise. Tyler backed her against the wall, fitting his hard body to her softer one. "Have I admitted yet that I'm in love with you, Katie Cat?" he asked.

Euphoria welled in her. "Maybe once or twice," she said, gazing deep into his gold-brown eyes and loving him so much her heart threatened to burst.

He raised his eyebrows waiting. "This is where you say something back," he prompted, "even though I've heard it before."

"Oh, sorry. I was caught up in the moment. I love you too, T-Rex," she replied.

He growled low in his throat. "You know what it does to me when you call me that," he warned, lowering his lips over hers.

But then the elevator chimed, and the doors swept open at their floor. Katie broke off the kiss and squirmed free. Now was not the time for them to get carried away. "Let me see your walk again," she said, backing down the hall ahead of him.

"Can I pull off a sexy swagger?" he asked, trying for a little bounce and making her laugh.

She worked their room key out of her back pocket. "Absolutely."

Not a sound came from behind their door, but then again SEALs were trained to be utterly silent. She stuck the key into the lock and pushed the door open. The room stood in semi-darkness with the curtains pulled.

Bronco stuck his nose out to greet them, but Tyler shot out a hand to prevent Katie from entering. "Wait a minute. Who pulled the curtains?"

"I did," Katie reassured him. "Bronco wouldn't let anyone in, would you buddy?"

Tyler relented, but his expression remained wary as he entered the room ahead of her, flicking on the light. He waded cautiously into the living area, signaling for Katie to stay behind him.

Without warning a dark figure stepped out of the bedroom door. "Surprise!"

Another man leapt off the floor from behind the couch and two others slipped out from behind the drawn drapes.

Katie studied Tyler's reaction to finding his former teammates in their roomy suite. "What the—?" He swung a startled look at her. "Did you know they were in here?"

"She invited us, man." The swarthy god of a man who'd hidden in their bedroom crossed the room and threw both arms around him.

Katie's throat closed up as Tyler returned his teammate's fierce embrace. *This must be Sam*, she concluded, the one she'd made arrangements with after a long and frustrating attempt to find him. SEALs truly were private people, and virtually invisible at that.

Sam finally released Tyler so he could greet the others.

"Bronco." He turned toward the man with sun-streaked hair, thumping his back as they exchanged a hearty embrace. "You know I named my dog after you, right?"

"I saw that on his collar," drawled the warrior with dancing blue eyes and a wicked grin. "You must have missed me."

"Hardly. He annoyed me the same way you do. Hey, Bullfrog," he said, holding out a hand to the tallest of the four, a man with a compassionate and intelligent expression. "Haiku," he added, shaking the Asian man's hand with gusto. "Damn, it's good to see you guys."

"You look good, Tyler," Bullfrog declared.

An aura of unquestioning camaraderie and boundless energy filled the room.

"Thank you. I feel good. Where's Cooper?" he

asked.

"Couldn't come," Sam answered with a grimace. "Your platoon just headed back to Malaysia to avenge you and to grab Haji once and for all."

"I thought Echo Platoon was going to do that."

"We were." Sam grimaced. "But then we were asked to recover the daughter of an oil tycoon instead, and Echo Platoon went without us."

"Damn," Tyler swore, regarding him closely. "What was that like?"

"I'll tell you about it some time," Sam promised.

Just then Tyler seemed to remember her. He swiveled toward Katie, beckoning her closer and putting an arm around her. "Guys, I want you to meet the reason for my resurrection. This is the beautiful Katie Crowley. She trains therapy dogs like this mutt here."

Sam stuck his hand out. "We spoke on the phone," he reminded her. "Thanks for taking good care of our brother here."

"Thank you for coming," she replied. Just as she thought it might, the support of Tyler's former teammates had obviously cheered him.

"Katie's going to marry me one day," Tyler interjected, drawing her startled gaze. They'd only been together for a month, and yet the declaration thrilled her more than it caught her off guard.

"Whoa, did you just propose?" Bronco the

SEAL demanded, looking back and forth between them.

"No, I don't have a ring yet," Tyler said with a shrug. "I just wanted you guys to know that this is serious."

"And how do you feel about that?" Bronco asked Katie, extending an imaginary mike.

She laughed at his antics. "I'm looking forward to it," she honestly replied.

Marrying Tyler Rexall! Only in her wildest teenage dreams could she have predicted that would happen.

"Well, now that introductions are over," Sam inserted briskly, "we can still catch the second half of the UFC championship, Velasquez is taking on that guy from Denmark."

Tyler responded enthusiastically. "Where's the remote control?" He found it on top of the television.

"What is UFC?" Katie asked, mystified, as SEALs scrambled for the limited seats.

"It's the Ultimate Fighting Championship—mixed martial arts." He sent her a pleading look. "Do you mind?"

"Of course not." She grinned at the lot of them—nothing but overgrown boys. "You guys have fun. I'll take Bronco for a walk and look for popcorn."

As she clipped on Bronco's leash, Tyler located the sport's channel featuring the event. Then he chased Katie to the door.

"Hey," he said, following her into the hall and leaving the door cracked. Catching her face in both hands, he stared into her eyes. "That was the nicest thing anyone's ever done for me, Katie Cat. I don't know what I ever did to deserve you."

Joy blossomed inside her. "You're welcome," she replied. "By the way, I'm going to hold you to your prediction."

"The one about us getting married?"

"That's the one."

"Not a problem," he assured her. Lowering his mouth over hers, he sealed his promise with the world's sweetest kiss.

Coming in August

DANGER CLOSE

ECHO PLATOON SERIES BOOK #1

THE SOUND OF running water preceded the feel of a large hand sliding under the back of her head, cradling it as he helped her to lift her shoulders. A paper cup touched her lips. "Here, take a sip, ma'am. It'll help."

The respectful term made her think of the military. As she swallowed a soothing draught, Maddy cracked her eyes and assessed her Good Samaritan through her lashes.

Definitely military, she confirmed. He was darkly handsome, thirtyish. Dried blood crusted the underside of his swollen nose. Dark green eyes regarded her with brooding intensity.

"Who are you?" she croaked, as he lowered her head and untangled his fingers from her hair.

"Lieutenant Sam Sasseville," he introduced himself. "This is Bronco, my chief," he added gesturing to the second man who wore a baseball cap over his burnished locks. Blue eyes shone out of an unnaturally bronzed face.

"Pleasure," said Bronco with a familiar chuckle.

Those blue eyes. That laugh. She'd met these

men before. A wave of alarm rolled belatedly through her. "Where am I?" she demanded, coming up on her elbows to assess the small, sterile space. Even that small movement made her want to lie back down and close her eyes, but she didn't. "How did I get here?"

"You're aboard the *Harry S. Truman,* currently in the Gulf of Mexico," the lieutenant said, in a tentative manner. "We're SEALs. We were tasked to recover you from Matamoros. Your father must have friends in high places," he tacked on unnecessarily.

A muted roar filled Maddy's ears. She started to sit up all the way, kicking off her blanket in order to stand, but the lieutenant laid a heavy hand on her shoulder, pushing her shoulder toward the pillow.

Another memory stirred. Something violent and frightening.

"You shouldn't move," he said.

"Don't touch me!"

He snatched his hand back as she sorted through the rush of emotions.

Ignoring his cautionary statement, Maggie sat up carefully. The room went into a slow spin and then subsided. "So my father is the reason I'm here," she deduced, putting the pieces together.

"Yes," both men said simultaneously.

Damn it, Daddy. "And you—you what?—you

slipped into the school while I slept and you grabbed me?" Surely her father would not have condoned such underhanded measures.

"Affirmative," said the lieutenant, but his inscrutable expression suggested there was more.

"Why can't I remember?"

"We, uh, we had to subdue you," he stiffly confessed.

The blue-eyed chief looked down at the floor, his lips crimped.

He was trying not to laugh, Maddy realized, outraged. The faces of Imelda, Graciela, Mercedes, and the other dozen girls at *El Santuario* flashed before her eyes. If they hadn't realized she was gone yet, they soon would. Her stomach cramped in anguish as she envisioned their confusion, followed by their terror when they realized how Maddy's desertion would impact them.

"What have you done?" she cried, directing her dismay at her father foremost, then glaring at the two men standing near her. "What have you done?" she repeated. "Those girls aren't safe without me!"

Lt. Sassville's mouth firmed with what might have been remorse. His companion—what was his name? Bronco?—clapped him on the shoulder.

"It's all you, sir," he stated with confidence. Then he nodded in her direction. "Feel better soon, ma'am." He backed swiftly out of the hatch behind him, leaving Maddy to direct her fury at just one man.

In a matter of days—maybe a week if they were lucky—every girl in the school would be preyed upon by a man, her innocence forcibly taken from her. The knowledge lodged in Maddy's throat like a pill, too big and bitter to swallow.

Dropping her face in her hands, she hid her devastation. A tide of degradation was overtaking Mexico, and she was no longer there to deflect it.

"Go away," she begged wanting desperately to be alone, to sulk, and to reconsider her options.

But the SEAL didn't move, not even when the pain in her chest doubled. "Why are you still here?" she raged, lifting her face from her hands. She couldn't grieve with him here in the room.

At first, his only answer was silence. But then he broke it, speaking in a condescending tone that made her eyes widen. "You realize you would've ended up raped or murdered if you'd stayed around much longer," he pointed out.

She glared at him. "How does that concern you?"

"Concern me?" He gave a purely Hispanic shrug. "It doesn't. I don't give a damn what might have happened to you." Except that his irate, protective tone said otherwise.

Stung by his antagonism, all she could do was

stare at him with her mouth open.

He took a step toward her, planting his hands on the edge of the bed and leaning down until his dark green eyes looked straight into her blue ones, and his scent stole over her. "I *should* be halfway around the world right now, hunting down high-value targets, not wasting my time protecting the daughter of an oil tycoon." His tone made his resentment obvious.

Memories bombarded Maddy, flickering through her mind so quickly she could scarcely get a read on them. Silhouettes emerged out of the darkness.

"You attacked me," she recalled, seeing a vision of him hauling back her mosquito netting.

He straightened like she'd slapped him in the face. "No way." He pointed a long finger at her. "I told you exactly who we were, and you resisted us, remember?"

All she remembered was him grabbing her out of the window and throwing her atop her bed. "You mauled me on my mattress," she added, remembering how she'd fought back.

"No," he exclaimed, shaking his head vehemently.

But a touch to the knot swelling just above her eyebrows confirmed the accuracy of her statement. She sent him an accusing glare. "Yes, you did."

"No. *You* tried escaping out the window," he insisted, his expression growing sterner by the moment. "And then you went crazy. Look what you did to my nose!"

She eyed his swollen nose ridge with a smidgen of satisfaction. Without the flaw, the man was simply too handsome for his own good. "Serves you right for scaring me half to death," she said, dismayed by her behavior. But his was worse.

His chest expanded and his hands clenched. "What the hell were you thinking ignoring a mandatory evacuation?"

Maddy bristled. "I was thinking that I was protecting innocent lives. What was I supposed to do? Just abandon those girls? How dare you lecture me for doing what you do every day, you overbearing hypocrite!"

The epithet sent his eyebrows winging toward his hairline. A disbelieving laugh escaped him and he unclenched his hands. "You couldn't begin to do what I do, Miss Scott," he countered, propping them on his hips with a smirk of confidence on his lips.

Maddy narrowed her eyes. Fury pounded through her. No man had ever put her back up in so short a time. "I never said I can do *exactly* what you do, Lieutenant. But I will risk my life for a cause that I believe in. In that sense, we're exactly alike."

His smile faded abruptly. "We are nothing alike," he insisted, his gaze sliding over her.

She sat up straighter, angling her chin at him.

"Oh, I see. SEALs don't protect the weak and combat corruption?"

She thought she had him bested when he paused for the barest second. "No," he finally countered. "We kill the enemy, Miss Scott. That's the difference between us." He tapped his broad chest. "I'm not a potential victim." He pointed at her. "*You* are."

More by
MARLISS MELTON

NAVY SEAL TEAM 12 SERIES

Forget Me Not

In the Dark

Time to Run

Next to Die

Don't Let Go

Too Far Gone

Show No Fear

Long Gone, A Novella

Code of Silence, A Novella

TASKFORCE TRILOGY

The Protector

The Guardian

The Enforcer

About the Author

Marliss Melton is the author of a dozen counterterrorist/romantic suspense stories, including a 7-book Navy SEALs series, a counterterrorist Taskforce Trilogy, two novellas and two short stories. She relies on her experience as a military spouse and on her many contacts in the Spec Ops and Intelligence communities to pen realistic and heartfelt stories about America's elite warriors and fearless agency heroes. Daughter of a U.S. foreign officer, Melton grew up in various countries overseas. She has taught English, Spanish, ESL, and Linguistics at the College of William and Mary, her alma mater. She lives near Virginia Beach with her husband, young daughter, and four college-aged children. Be sure to "friend" Marliss on Facebook!

Visit www.marlissmelton.com for more information.

CPSIA information can be obtained at www.ICGtesting.com
Printed in the USA
LVOW12s1613070814

398030LV00020B/1349/P